MARILYN PAPPANO

has been blessed by family—her husband, their son, his lovely wife and a grandson who is almost certainly the most beautiful and talented baby in the world—and friends, along with a writing career that's made her one of the luckiest people around.

LINDA CONRAD

A bestselling author of more than twenty-five books, Linda has received numerous industry awards, among them a National Reader's Choice Award, a Maggie Award, a Write Touch Readers' Award and an *RT Book Reviews* Reviewers' Choice Award. To contact Linda, read more about her books or to sign up for her newsletter and/or contests, go to her Web site at www.LindaConrad.com.

LORETH ANNE WHITE

Born and raised in southern Africa, Loreth now lives in Whistler, a ski resort in the moody British Columbian Coast Mountain range. It's a place of vast wilderness, larger-than-life characters, epic adventure and romance—the perfect place to escape reality. It's no wonder she was inspired to abandon a sixteen-year career as a journalist to escape into a world of romance fiction filled with dangerous men and adventurous women.

For a peek into her world visit her Web site, www.lorethannewhite.com. She'd love to hear from you.

MARILYN PAPPANO, LINDA CONRAD & LORETH ANNE WHITE

Covert Christmas

ROMANTIC
SUSPENSE

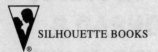 SILHOUETTE BOOKS

Recycling programs for this product may not exist in your area.

ISBN-13: 978-0-373-27697-4

COVERT CHRISTMAS

Copyright © 2010 by Harlequin Books S.A.

The publisher acknowledges the copyright holders of the individual works as follows:

OPEN SEASON
Copyright © 2010 by Marilyn Pappano

SECOND-CHANCE SHERIFF
Copyright © 2010 by Linda Lucas Sankpill

SAVING CHRISTMAS
Copyright © 2010 by Loreth Beswetherick

This edition published by arrangement with Harlequin Books S.A.

For questions and comments about the quality of this book please contact us at Customer_eCare@Harlequin.ca.

® and TM are trademarks of Harlequin Books S.A., used under license. Trademarks indicated with ® are registered in the United States Patent and Trademark Office, the Canadian Trade Marks Office and in other countries.

Visit Silhouette Books at www.eHarlequin.com

Printed in U.S.A.

CONTENTS

Dear Reader,

Before this holidays get rolling, fortify yourself with October's heart-thumping romances from Silhouette Romantic Suspense.

Three of your favorite authors—Marilyn Pappano, Linda Conrad and Loreth Anne White—contribute fabulous mayhem-filled holiday stories in *Covert Christmas* (#1627). Don't miss the yuletide excitement! Follow THE COLTONS OF MONTANA in the latest romance, *Dr. Colton's High-Stakes Fiancée* (#1628), by Cindy Dees. Two lovers reunite but will a tornado—and a more human threat—get in the way of happiness? Next is Karen Whiddon's *Profile for Seduction* (#1629), which is part of her miniseries THE CORDASIC LEGACY. Here, two agents chase down an escaped serial killer—and try to resist their smoldering passion. In Beth Cornelison's *The Bride's Bodyguard* (#1630), the second book in THE BANCROFT BRIDES, a reluctant bride gets swept off her feet by a hunky military man who's determined to protect her from a virulent evil. You won't be able to put these stories down.

Each month, Silhouette Romantic Suspense will take your breath away! Become a fan of our books on www.Facebook.com and visit us at www.eHarlequin.com. Have a wonderful holiday season and happy reading!

Sincerely,

Patience Smith
Senior Editor

OPEN SEASON

Marilyn Pappano

To my grandson, Cameron, who still believes in Santa Claus; my son, Brandon, and his lovely wife, Bobbi; and my husband, Bob. For making Christmas that much more special. I love you guys!

Chapter 1

With one last glance over her shoulder, Natalia Parker turned off the sidewalk onto an overgrown path and gave a sigh of relief. She always felt exposed on Augusta's streets, but here, at the ancient house where she rented the upstairs apartment, azaleas grown wild mostly hid her from sight.

A sharp wind cut through the narrow alley formed by house and fence, making her shiver. She'd gotten rid of her heavy clothes when she'd left Chicago, and the unusually frigid temperatures this week made her regret it.

As if she didn't have enough regrets already.

She reached the back of the house, resting one hand on the siding to balance as she stepped across the arching roots of a long-gone live oak. A plaster fairy sat on the rough-sawn stump, looking cold in the thin evening light. Clearing the roots and the corner, Natalia headed for the rickety stairs, her thoughts on warmth, security, hot cocoa and a movie.

Abruptly, awareness prickled down her neck. Danger. Her gaze swept the small yard, from fence to vine-covered fence, past a pine, an oak and a gum tree, before darting back to the oak.

In the shadows a lean figure stood motionless, his brown leather jacket and trousers practically blending into the bark. His stance was casual: one shoulder against the tree, one knee cocked. A knitted cap covered most of his long blond hair, and a beard stubbled his chin. For three and a half years, she'd seen him in her dreams. In her nightmares. And now here he was, in the flesh.

Josh Saldana.

He pushed away from the tree, taking a few steps into the light cast by the weak lamp outside her door, shoving his hands into his jacket pockets. "Hey, Nat."

His voice was low, his manner loose, but neither lessened the menace emanating from him. She'd known danger since she was a child. She sensed it, smelled it, tasted it, chilling the very air between them.

Cursing the mall job that forced her to go out with nothing more than a four-inch blade for protection, she gauged the distance to the stairs. She might make it halfway to the top before he caught her—maybe, with luck, all the way. But the door to her apartment would give with one good kick, and the only other exit was a fifteen-foot drop out the bedroom window. Her sole hope of escape was back the way she'd just come, to the street, to the open.

"What's wrong, Nat? Cat got your tongue?"

She locked gazes with him. His eyes were so blue, they defied description. Usually they were full of emotion: warm; heated; laughing; angry; gentle; mocking; deeply, darkly passionate. This evening they were blank.

How had he found her? Why had he bothered? To avenge the wrongs she'd done him? Payback was a bitch, he'd always said.

She'd had enough payback to last a lifetime. She wasn't looking for any more.

Willing herself to give no hint of her intent, she suddenly lunged, spinning around, racing for the corner. She had a few seconds, max, before he reacted, and he was bigger, faster. Given half a chance, he would be on her before she reached the sidewalk.

Her leap carried her over the bigger tree roots, but she stubbed her toe on a small one, sending her skittering for balance. She'd almost found it when Josh slammed into her from behind. Her landing was hard, sending her glasses flying, rushing her breath out with a grunt, forcing her face to the ground. The rich scents of earth and decaying leaves filled her lungs, threatening to choke her, before the pressure on her back eased.

"Gee, Nat, you make a man think you're not happy to see him," he drawled in her ear. "And here I've been looking forward to this for so long."

She'd wondered if she would ever see him again—had let herself, when she was weak, fantasize that he would come looking for her, that he still wanted her, that he might even love her. He'd said the words plenty of times, but saying something didn't make it so.

Just as not saying it didn't make that true, either.

Tentatively, she pushed, but couldn't budge him. He was lean, far thinner than when she'd last seen him, but he was strong. "What do you want?" Her voice sounded rusty. She got through her days at work with little conversation, and there was no one to talk to outside the job. There hadn't been since she'd fled Copper Lake, Georgia, seven months ago.

He moved, rising to his knees, his thighs still pressed tight against hers. "You're kidding, right? What do I *want*? You can ask that?"

The disdain in his voice sent a shiver through her unmatched by the frigid air. He'd never spoken to her like that, not once since the hot Chicago day they'd met. He'd thought it luck that they'd both gone to pick up their cars at the garage at the same time. Obviously he now knew there'd been nothing lucky about their meeting. She'd gone there on orders from her boss, had waited three hours for the man whose face she'd memorized from the photos Patrick Mulroney had shown her. She'd gone with an agenda, and it had led to an attempt—two—on Josh's life.

She deserved his disdain. What she'd done had been unforgivable.

Apparently tiring of waiting for her answer, he stood up, grabbed hold of her arm and hauled her to her feet. His grip never lessened, not as he bent to retrieve her glasses, not as he turned her toward the back of the house again and pushed her along ahead of him. "I've waited a long time for this conversation. I'd rather have it inside, where I'm not freezing my ass off."

"We've got nothing to talk about." Her denial sounded weak, even to her, and the only response it brought from him was a snort.

Given no choice, she climbed the stairs, seventeen of them, to the three-by-four-foot stoop. The screen door creaked when she opened it, and the key jingled when she took it from her pocket. Mrs. Johnstone, almost as creaky and faded as her house, had given Natalia the key ring, painted gaudy gold and dangling red and green jingle bells. *It'll get you in the holiday spirit*, she'd said sourly.

The door swung open into quiet darkness. The apartment was as grim as the rest of Natalia's life: a tiny living room, a tinier kitchen, a bedroom and a bathroom. The floors were wood, their finish worn off in the past hundred years, and the furniture was cast-off: love seat, glider, coffee table, chrome-and-vinyl dinette with two chairs, double bed with a mattress like lumpy straw. Her only possessions, a flat-screen television and endless cartons of DVDs, stood out from the rest, modernity amidst antiquity.

Josh stepped inside, closed and locked the door, then released her arm. He looked around the apartment, his mouth settling into a thin line, then fixed his gaze on her. Was it the rooms she called home he found lacking, or her? "Nice place," he remarked flatly.

With a whoosh, she let out her breath, then pulled off her gloves, tossing them on the love seat. Her jacket and scarf followed. "I like it," she replied, her voice as airy as if she were simply making polite conversation. "All the comforts of home, close to work—"

"Cheap."

Deep inside she flinched, then silently chastised herself. Josh's approval didn't matter to her anymore. She'd lived in nicer places, sure, but there'd been plenty that were much worse. Surroundings didn't matter. The expensive condo the Mulroneys had provided her with in Chicago may have been more comfortable, but it hadn't made what she was doing any less despicable. This apartment might be shabby, but she was paying for it herself, with money earned honestly.

And God knew Josh wasn't one to criticize living dishonestly.

"Can I have my glasses?"

He glanced at the metal frames a moment before placing them in her palm. They were cold against her skin, but she swore for an instant heat radiated from them before he drew back.

She slid the glasses on, bringing the room into sharp focus, then asked the question burning in the back of her mind. "How did you find me?" *And why?* Because he needed answers? Because he wanted to punish her?

Maybe, just maybe, because he still—just a little bit—cared about her?

Then he brought his gaze back to hers, and scorn washed over her. "It was surprisingly easy. All I had to do was listen when you talked."

The answer puzzled her. She'd been hiding from someone or other since she was a kid. She didn't make unconscious slips; she never told anyone more than they needed to know. Could she have told him something important, something true, without remembering it?

Memories of sex, hot, steamy, wicked, warmed her from the inside out. She'd been lucky to remember her name by the time he'd finished touching her, kissing her, making her feel. Yeah, she could have told him something.

Shoving his hands into his pockets, he strolled around the perimeter of the two rooms, pausing to glance out the kitchen window, barely a foot square, situated above the equally small sink, then doing the same at the living room window, also small. Just checking out the view? Or had the last three years taught him the value of remaining constantly on alert?

Though people could surprise you even when you were alert. She practically slept with her eyes open, and yet Josh had managed to get within twenty feet of her before she knew it.

Satisfied with what he'd seen—or hadn't seen—outside, he returned to stand halfway between her and the door. He was loose-limbed, deceptively at ease as he stared at her. She held herself motionless. She wouldn't let him know that the fine hairs on her neck were prickling, that electricity danced along her nerves and anxiety threatened to explode in her belly if she didn't move.

The heat rumbled on, loud, sending puffs of warm air into the room, making her realize how cold she was. She wanted to grab her jacket and bundle up again, but she couldn't force herself into action.

Finally he opened his mouth, to ask questions she couldn't answer, to make accusations she couldn't deny, but the words that vibrated in the air didn't come from him.

"Natalia Parker! Josh Saldana! We've got you surrounded! Come out with your hands up!"

The bellow came from the porch and was followed by a braying laugh. Josh might not have recognized the voice right away, but he knew the laugh. He'd heard it too many times when he'd worked for the Mulroney brothers, two of Chicago's more successful mobsters. Mickey Davison was six feet two, two hundred and twenty pounds of pure muscle, dumber than dirt and loyal to the death to his bosses. Loyal, at least, to other people's deaths, or so it was rumored.

And where Davison went, so did Clive Leeves. Davison was the brawn; Leeves was both brain and brawn.

The banging threatened to splinter the flimsy door on its hinges. "We know you're in there. Open the door or I'll huff and puff and blow the house in." Another donkey laugh underscored the threat.

Josh grabbed Natalia's hand and headed for the bedroom, slowing only enough to let her snatch up her coat and gloves from the sofa. He'd checked the exterior of the apartment while he'd waited for her to come home and had seen the only way out besides the front door. It was a long drop to cold, hard ground—no bushes, thank God—but maybe they could make it without breaking a bone or two.

The odds that they could come out of a face-to-face with Davison and Leeves with so little damage were squarely between nil and none.

In the bedroom he let go of Natalia, pushed aside the curtain and shoved the window up, then turned to find her on her knees, rummaging under the bed. "What are you doing?" he demanded as the banging at the door deepened in tone. Davison was no longer using his fist but his foot. If the door didn't give with the next kick, the jamb would. Either way, they were screwed if they didn't get out now.

"I need this." She hauled a black duffel from under the bed, then shoved something into her jacket pocket as she stood.

A pistol. Josh had known for seven months that she was a liar, a traitor, a spy. He knew she'd been involved in the hits on him, when Joe had twice almost died in Josh's place. He knew she was one of the bad guys. But it shook him to see her with a gun. Who the hell—what the hell—was she, and how had he fallen in love with her without even knowing her?

From the next room came the sound of splintering wood and shrieking nails forced from their hold. Josh stepped aside as Natalia tossed the bag out the window, then climbed onto the sill. "I'll give you a hand."

She didn't argue but slipped backward out the window, her legs dangling in the air. She wrapped her fingers tightly around his, and he leaned out as far as he could, feet wide apart to brace himself. When he'd stretched to the limit, he let go.

She hit the ground with a grunt, snatched up the duffel and scrambled out of his way.

His landing was harder, jarring his bones all the way up to the top of his skull. For a moment he lay dazed, teeth rattling, ears ringing. Then she was pulling at him—*Get up, get up!*—and Davison was leaning out the window above, weapon in hand.

"Hey, Saldana." Davison's voice was nasally for so big a guy. "Long time, no see."

Natalia heaved, and Josh willed every ache in his body to move with her, rolling to the side an instant before the bullet bit into the ground where he'd been. He got to his feet, staggered a few yards until he shook off the impact, then grabbed her hand and ran.

The yard on this side of the house was even more overgrown than the other. Crape myrtles tangled together, big ones sending out runners to form little ones, and weeds covered the ground. Natalia led the way, ducking branches, weaving around saplings, pausing when they reached the sidewalk.

"Do you have a car?"

He shook his head. He hadn't held a steady job since he'd gone on the run with the Feds three years ago. Since parting company with them last spring, he'd worked odd jobs, gambled and stolen to make his way. He couldn't afford a car, couldn't register a tag in his name or buy insurance.

A ruckus came from the back of the house: feet pounding down the stairs, angry voices, creative cursing.

"This way," she said, and they ran along the cracked sidewalk to the north. They turned at the first corner, and she skidded to a stop.

Parked along the curb was a black SUV with tinted windows. It looked like a thousand other SUVs until he noticed what she'd seen right away: the Illinois tag. Releasing his hand, she yanked up the left leg of her jeans, removed a blade from a leather sheath and, in swift, powerful movements, sank it into first the right rear tire, then the front one.

A knife, a gun and Natalia. He couldn't reconcile the

weapons with the woman he'd thought he knew. She'd been so delicate, so feminine, so in need of him. He'd wanted to take care of her, to protect her.

What a joke. She didn't need protection, and she'd damn sure never needed him.

The hissing of compressed air mingled with the buzz of the streetlamps. He guessed the temperature was about thirty degrees, not bad if you were dressed for it, which neither of them were. When the Feds had hustled him out of Chicago, he'd taken little enough with him: one suitcase of clothes, a single family photo, a new identity and a boatload of guilt.

He'd left all of that behind when he'd escaped protective custody, except for the picture and the guilt.

With the knife resheathed, Natalia started running again and he followed a few paces behind. She'd slung the duffel strap over her head and one shoulder and held the bag with one hand to keep it from bumping against her. At the next corner, she turned right again, doubling back toward her house, then darting into an alley halfway down the block. They continued to zigzag from alley to street and back again. His lungs were burning, his legs protesting, when she moved into the deep shadows behind an unlit office building and stopped, crouching to catch her breath.

He bent at the waist, hands resting on his thighs, and gulped a lungful of cold air. His scalp was itchy under the wool cap, and sweat was trickling down his spine. His brother was the athlete in the family. Josh had always preferred less strenuous pastimes, like counting cards or perfecting a con.

Or, he remembered, glancing at Natalia, charming a woman right out of her clothes.

She'd been incredible out of her clothes.

She'd been incredible in them.

She'd made him think—

Grimly he shut down that avenue of thought *fast*. If he focused too much on what he'd thought, how he'd felt, he might lose sight of the fact that Davison and Leeves were somewhere out there looking for him, and they weren't wanting to relive the good ol' days.

Little more than a blur in the darkness, she set the duffel on the ground, then the zipper rasped open. A tiny penlight she'd produced from somewhere illuminated the contents, and he crouched to get a better view of what she'd considered too important to leave behind.

It was her version of an emergency kit. There were a couple sets of clothes, all in dark colors. A pair of black running shoes. Travel-size toiletries. A box of ammunition. And what she was after right now: a wad of cash. If it was all twenties, like the bill visible, he'd put it at about two grand. Not bad for an emergency getaway.

She flattened the money, then shoved half into her left front jeans pocket, the other half into the right pocket, before going still, head cocked to one side. Josh listened, too, and heard footsteps approaching. It wasn't the solid thud of rubber-soled sneakers, but more of a slap. Dress shoes. No matter what the job, Clive Leeves always wore suits and pricey loafers. The clothes made the man, he claimed.

Other than the shadows, there was no hiding place—no trees nearby, no convenient Dumpster, not even a car to hunker down behind. They had only two options: run like hell or get inside the building.

Natalia fumbled in the duffel again, finding a small zippered case. She tossed the duffel to him, then jerked the zipper open, the sound harsh on the night air, as she trotted to the nearest door.

The case held lock picks, he saw when he joined her against the brick building. A knife, a gun, plenty of cash and lock picks. She definitely didn't need him to take care of her.

Leeves was closer, visible in a streetlight half a block away, when the lock tumblers fell into place with a quiet click. Natalia opened the door wide enough to slip in, then closed it the instant Josh cleared the frame, locking it again.

Total darkness enveloped them. He could hear her breathing, slow and steady, and his own heart thumping, anything but steady. Somewhere a clock ticked, and the furnace hummed, then came the scuff of shoe sole on pavement. His breath caught, and he strained to separate real sound from the overwhelming magnification of the total blackness around him. Was that a footstep? A voice? A hand clasping the door knob?

The door rattled, and Josh's heartbeat skipped. Leeves muttered something before his footsteps faded into the distance. Josh slid to the floor. "Jeez."

The penlight came on again, cupped in the shelter of Natalia's hand, moving up to the corners and along the walls. "No cameras outside," she murmured. "None here."

Her fingers were pale, delicate. The first time they'd met, she had offered her hand, and he'd thought it soft, amazingly feminine—functional, of course, but more. He'd held it longer than he should have, had wondered how it might feel against his flesh, not just touching but stroking, caressing, arousing.

His wildest imaginings hadn't come close to reality.

The light and those talented fingers gestured away from the door. "Let's find a place where we can hide out for a while, at least until Leeves and Davison give up for the night."

Nodding though she couldn't see, he pushed to his feet and started moving, his right hand trailing along the wall for security. "Do you know where we are?"

"In general, yes. Do I know this building? No."

When the hall ended, she turned, passing several closed doors on the left—the side that would likely have windows—before easing open a door on the right. The beam of the flashlight panned across the room: a break room, small, the only window frosted and opening on the corridor, with tables and chairs, a sofa, a microwave and vending machines.

Josh closed the door, felt for a lock but didn't find one, then flipped on the lights. His eyes immediately narrowed in response to the brightness, but he forced them back open to take in the room. To stare blankly. "Damn, it looks like Santa's workshop exploded in here."

Everything was red and green or held something in those colors. An artificial tree against one wall was decked with red satin balls, and fake garlands with red velvet bows looped from one corner to the next. Fuzzy red stockings with white cuffs were taped to one wall, names spelled out in red glitter: Doris, Tom, Jimmie, Amy, Anna, April. A two-foot-tall Santa occupied the nearest table, with smaller versions, plus angels and reindeer, sitting on every other flat surface, and unlit red and green candles gave off the sickly scents of manufactured cinnamon and pine. All that was missing was music, and even that started when Natalia passed too close to one table.

Rudolph the Red-Nosed Reindeer, the faux Bambi at the table's center sang as its head bobbed and its nose flashed red.

Natalia fumbled with the reindeer, stopping the song mid-chorus, then stood in the sudden silence, arms hugged to her middle. She'd made a few efforts to change her appearance in the months since she'd left Copper Lake. Her hair gleamed a brassy red in place of the light brown that was natural, and instead of the super-short cut she'd favored, it brushed her shoulders, shaggy and uneven. She'd traded her colored contact lenses for glasses, which meant her eyes were the hazel she'd been born with instead of the violet, green or turquoise she'd preferred, and her clothing was baggy, dark, drab. Nothing that said *Look at me; I'm a pretty woman.*

The changes might have fooled someone else, but not Josh. He would've known her from a mile away. Hell, he was pretty sure he'd felt her presence long before he'd actually seen her.

Right now she looked about as happy as she had the first moment she'd recognized him in the yard outside her apartment, and he remembered abruptly that he was pissed with her. Hell, he'd passed pissed seven months ago, when he'd found out that she was one of the Mulroneys' people.

He pulled a chair from one of the tables and shoved it in her direction. "I've got an idea, Nat. Let's pass the time with a game of Twenty Questions. I'll ask, and you'll answer." He forced all the anger inside him into his next word, making it an order, a threat and a promise all in one.

"Sit."

Chapter 2

Natalia's hand trembled just the slightest bit, not enough for Josh to notice, before she wrapped her fingers around the back of the chair and pulled it nearer. She didn't sit, though, not right away. Sitting made a person subservient. It put her at a disadvantage, adding one additional movement to anything she did. "Like I said earlier, we have nothing to talk about."

Prowling the room, looking inside cabinets, he laughed. "Right. Just your lies, your deception, your dishonesty, your general lack of trustworthiness."

"Interesting insults, considering who's making them."

He shot a look at her over his shoulder. "I never lied to you. I never betrayed you."

Never, ever lied? So all those times you said 'I love you,' you meant it? But wanting to believe he'd felt something for her seemed pathetic, and asking for reassurance of it seemed really pathetic. "You never admitted to working for the Mulroneys."

"I never denied it, either." His expression was smug. "You never asked."

She hadn't, because she'd known before she'd met him. Patrick Mulroney had given her that information, along with plenty more, when he'd asked her to get close to Josh. He'd given her pictures, too, and she'd taken one look at them and been…

It didn't matter now that she'd been vulnerable enough to be infatuated or stupid enough to dream. She wasn't that woman anymore.

Wearily she sank into the chair and asked, "What do you want to know?"

At first he paid her question no mind, as if he'd known she would fold. As if it wasn't really that important to him. He continued to root through the cabinets, assembling a small cache on the countertop: containers of microwaveable soup, a sleeve of crackers, a canister of coffee. He popped the top off a tomato soup, stuck it in the microwave and set it, then started coffee brewing. Within five minutes, dinner was ready, and her question still hung in the air between them, as impossible to ignore as the Christmas trimmings around them.

With the meal on the table, he sat across from her, crumbled a handful of saltines into his soup, dusted his hands and fixed his gaze on her. "Why were you working for the Mulroneys?"

She crumbled crackers into her own soup and stirred until they disappeared beneath tiny chunks of vegetables and tomato-flavored broth. "Why were you?"

He shrugged. "Because that's what I did. I worked for people who gave me opportunities I couldn't find in the law-abiding world."

"That's what I did, too."

He didn't miss a beat. "Bullshit."

"You're saying women can't appreciate opportunities not found in a law-abiding world?"

"I'm saying you can't. You're about as Goody Two-shoes as they come."

Natalia practically choked. He knew now that she'd been working for the Mulroney brothers when they'd met. She'd been at least partly responsible for two attempts on his life. Even now, she was hiding out, working a minimum-wage job with twenty-eight-hundred dollars in cash stuffed in her pockets, a knife strapped to her ankle and a gun in her pocket, and he was calling her Goody Two-shoes? "You're delusional."

His expression didn't change as he asked again, "Why were you working for the Mulroneys?"

Lie or tell the truth. She'd done a lot of lying in the past few years. She could do so now. What difference would the truth make? None to her. Once he heard it, none to him. But it would make him move on and leave her alone. Again.

"I moved to Chicago about five months before we met." She'd been running scared, with one small bag holding everything she owned and thirty-seven bucks and change. Less than twenty-four hours after she'd arrived, she had been dragged into an alleyway, robbed, beaten and damn near raped. She wouldn't trust him with that detail, though. She didn't want his pity or, worse, his accusation that she'd make up such a lie.

"Right away I got mugged, and Patrick Mulroney rescued me. I had no money, no place to go, no one to turn to, so he offered to help. He let me stay in one of his apartments. He loaned me the money to get back on my feet. He even got me a job with a friend of his."

Josh's gaze raked over her, from the top of the shaggy red hair she hated over her ill-fitting clothes to her chunky boots. She knew he was remembering the expensive clothes she'd worn back then, the pricey car she'd driven…and the pretty, well-dressed prostitutes who contributed greatly to the Mulroneys' bottom line. The cynicism in his eyes echoed in his voice, cold and hard. "What kind of job?"

Her stomach muscles clenched. "Secretary. For a plumbing supply company." She'd earned about a tenth of what that expensive apartment must have cost each month, but she'd thought Patrick was helping her out of the kindness of his heart. She'd been so naive. Given the family she'd grown up with, how had she convinced herself that there were people with kindness in their hearts?

It was impossible to tell if Josh believed her. Though on

the surface he appeared as easygoing as ever, there was a subtle stiffness to his movements, born of anger, resentment, hostility—all the ugly emotions he'd never shown her in the past. "So you live off Patrick's generosity for a while, and one day he comes to you and says, 'It's time to pay up?'"

"No." Natalia would like to think such bluntness would have been enough to send her on the run again. Yes, she'd taken advantage of everything he'd offered, but she'd worked hard. She had paid back every penny of the cash he'd loaned her. She'd rarely driven the car he'd provided, and she had been saving to get her own place. She had intended to get back on her feet, in accordance with his original offer, and live on her own.

She had never guessed he had other plans.

"He came to me one day and said there was a guy who worked for him who was up to something. He didn't know if it was just stealing from the company, or using it to cover up something worse. He wanted someone to keep an eye on him—on you—but you knew everyone who worked for him. He asked if I would do this favor for him."

Again, it was impossible to tell if Josh believed her or thought she was lying to make herself sound less culpable. She wasn't trying to get rid of the guilt; it had become such an ingrained part of her that she wouldn't know how to live without it. She just wanted to answer his questions and get him out of her life because it had taken her too damn long to learn to live without him the first time, and she was older now. Wearier.

"And you owed him so much, you just couldn't tell him no."

She shrugged. Patrick Mulroney had been the first person in her life who'd cared. He'd truly saved her that night in the dimly lit alley. He'd restored her faith in people.

And he'd had an ulterior motive all along. Maybe he hadn't immediately seen her as a way to control Josh, but he'd known that someday, somehow, she would come in handy. All he'd had to do was show her a little kindness, and she'd been so grateful that she would have done anything he asked.

Even betray the man she'd fallen in love with.

"So spying on me, screwing with me, sleeping with me—that was all just payback for him taking care of you." He was trying to keep his voice level—she knew him well enough to recognize it—but there was an edge to it that he couldn't control. Anger? Disgust?

Hurt? Had she hurt him?

The thought had never occurred to her. She'd known he would hate her when he found out the truth, had known he would be angry at her betrayal. But hurt? He'd cared enough to be hurt?

A lump formed in her throat, forcing her to swallow hard. "It was a job. Just like every job you did for them." In the beginning, it hadn't even been that. A favor, Patrick had called it. A chance to repay the man who'd saved her, she'd thought. But after the Mulroneys' first try at killing Josh, it had become a mess she couldn't get out of.

Because she had made her usual check-in that day. She'd told them where to find him. By the time she'd realized that Patrick and his brother weren't merely protecting their business but trying to silence a witness against them, it had been too late. She'd been in it up to her pretty little neck, Sean Mulroney had pointed out.

"At least I didn't screw with people," Josh denied.

She shook off the melancholy hovering around her. "No, you just stole from them. Scammed them out of everything they owned. Lied, cheated, set them up and let them fall."

"I never pretended—" A tinge of crimson crept into his cheeks as he broke off. Josh Saldana feeling guilty. Who had known he was capable?

"To be someone you weren't? To feel something you didn't?" She snorted. "Right. You were always pretending, Josh, always saying and doing the things to get what you wanted."

He stared at her a long time, his mouth thinned, then shook his head. "I never took anything they couldn't afford to lose."

She stood up and tossed her soup container, spoon and coffee cup into the trash. "So you were a thief and a con man, but you had standards." She paused for effect, then quietly added, "Your parents must be so proud."

It was a low blow, based on things he'd told her in confidence. She'd thought at the time that he'd told her all his secrets, except for dealing with the Feds to get himself out of trouble. She'd had to learn that one from the newspapers.

His face paled, and the veins in his neck tightened. He stood, too, and gathered his trash, then passed close to her. After dropping it into the stainless-steel can, he turned, mere inches away. His gaze met hers—no hiding the disdain now—and his lip curled into a sneer. "Go to hell, Natalia."

All her life it would have been a short trip, except for those few months in Chicago with him. All her life she'd figured there must be some reason she deserved such grief. A person couldn't be as consistently down and out as she'd been without a reason, unless it—she—was God's idea of a joke.

But sometimes she saw a flicker of hope—when she'd fallen in love with Josh. When she'd gained acceptance and friendship from his brother, Joe. For just an instant when she'd recognized Josh in the yard this evening. Maybe there really was such a thing as Christmas miracles.

Go to hell, Natalia.

But not for her.

She took a breath, ready for more questions, to be alone again, to give up the faintest flickers of hope that her life might change. "What else do you want to know?"

As if she'd answered that question adequately.

Josh stifled a snort as he stared at her. She'd aged more than the last three years could account for. Guilt, he hoped. After what she'd done, she didn't deserve to go on with her life as if nothing had happened.

Of course, he'd aged, too. Nothing had brought that home as clearly as his brief visit with his brother on the way to Augusta. For thirty-some years, they'd been virtually identical in looks. Now the resemblance between them was more of a family thing and less a twin thing. Instead of the seven-minute head start he had on Joe, he looked a hard seven years older.

"Was anything you ever said true?" It wasn't one of the real questions he wanted to ask. Not *Why?* Or *Did you ever feel anything for me?* Or *How could you do it?* Even *Did you regret it?* But it was a start.

"Practically everything." She sounded as tired as she looked, but he was way beyond feeling sympathetic.

"Everything but the important stuff."

She raised one hand to gesture around her. "You found me. Obviously I told you something important." A pause. "What was it?"

He could keep the answer from her. Yeah, it was petty, but it would soothe his ego to know he had something she wanted. It was a little bit of power for him, when all the power before had been hers.

But he was trying to change, right? Trying to become someone different. Better. Someone people weren't trying to kill. Someone his brother and their parents might someday respect.

"When you were a kid, your grandmother lived in Augusta. Over by the mall, a couple blocks off the Bobby Jones Expressway. You visited her in the summer. It was the only place you ever felt…"

The memory formed in his mind, as clear as if it had just happened. She'd been naked in his bed, limp and sleepy and talking in a drowsy murmur. It was the only place she'd ever felt wanted, she'd whispered, and he—he'd hurt for her. He had wanted to hold her tighter, to promise her that he would want her forever, but before he'd said the words, she had begun to snore softly in his arms. He had lain awake that whole night, holding her, facing feelings for her that were too big, too intense, but feeling them all the same.

If she'd remembered any part of the conversation the next day, she'd given no hint.

Now her face was flushed. She might not remember telling him something so personal, but clearly she had an idea what she might have said. Stiffly she moved away and crossed her arms. "So you came to Augusta and…what?"

"Got lucky." That was what he was known for: being the luckiest son of a bitch that ever lived. "You and your grandmother walked to the mall every day to buy cinnamon rolls. Even when you were ten, she still made you hold her hand when you crossed Gordon Highway. So I've been hanging out."

And he'd gotten lucky. The bakery was only a hundred feet from the storefront where she worked wrapping Christmas gifts. Yesterday afternoon he'd spotted her, buying a cinnamon roll for lunch, and last night he'd followed her home, but he had been so pissed that he'd put off confronting her until today.

"Lucky," she scoffed. "You brought Davison and Leeves to my door."

"No way. Nobody followed me."

"So it's a coincidence that they showed up minutes after you?"

"The entire United States Marshals Service, along with numerous local and state authorities, are looking for me, and you think Davison and Leeves found me?" He shook his head. "I figure they already knew where you were and were just waiting for me to show up. When I did, they crawled out of the gutter."

"Why would they think you'd show up?"

He gave her a long, dry look. She was a beautiful woman. She'd seduced him, lied to him, set him up and almost gotten him—or, at least, his twin—killed. And he'd been stupid in love with her. Everyone had known he would go looking for her, except, apparently, her.

Her hair gleamed in the overhead light when she shook her head, the color easy and flirty and so not her. "I would have known if someone was following me."

"You were still working for the Mulroneys when you moved to Copper Lake, and they were watching you then. When you ran, you didn't go far. They were probably right behind you."

She continued to shake her head. "I would have known."

Her self-confidence reminded him of himself—and, yeah, he'd been wrong a few times. He was about to point that out—*Like you knew I was there waiting for you?*—when the lights in the corridor came on and a woman's voice sounded from down the hall.

"I left the wine on my desk. I'll just be a minute." Purposeful footsteps muffled by carpet headed their way.

Josh's gaze darted around the room, locating the only hiding place: a small corner where vending machines stood at right angles to each other. Natalia grabbed her bag and tossed it on top of one machine, then headed for the light switch. He caught her hand as a shadow fell across the frosted glass, shoved her into the narrow opening, then joined her.

The steps stopped an instant before the door swung open. "Sheesh, Anna," the intruder grumbled. "It's part of your job. Rinse the coffeepot, unplug the machine and turn out the lights. Is it too much to ask that you actually do it?"

As the woman came into sight, Josh pressed back, forcing Natalia against the wall. The woman wore a long black skirt with a sequined top—formal wear for the grandmotherly type. Perfume floated on the air, a heavy floral, and diamond studs, a carat or so, decent cut, nice sparkle, twinkled in her ears.

Still grumbling, she laid a purse next to the fake reindeer, emptied the coffeepot and rinsed it, then unplugged the machine. She swept the room with her gaze, probably looking for anything else she could blame on Anna, then picked up her bag. Only a few steps away, she pivoted and turned back, waving her hand in front of the reindeer. "You turned off Rudolph, too? I guess I'm lucky you didn't throw him in the trash."

After she fiddled with the reindeer a moment, it burst into song and, smiling with smug satisfaction, she started to the door again. "I'm your Secret Santa, Anna. Forget the present I already bought. I know exactly what you're gonna be getting tomorrow."

She switched off the light, then closed the door behind her.

Rudolph's nose blinked crazily as it continued to sing, drowning out the sound of her footsteps.

Josh remained motionless, his breathing slow and shallow. Natalia was so still and quiet that if he didn't feel her warmth against his back, he wouldn't even know she was there.

The reindeer reached the end of its tune in time for Josh to pick out the fading sound of footsteps again. An instant later, the hall lights went off and the break room fell into near darkness, the only illumination coming from the vending machines.

Natalia let out a soft sigh and wriggled to one side, putting an inch or two of space between them. He turned, blocking the escape from their hiding place, facing her. She met his scrutiny without blinking, giving him back the same steady look.

The wine woman's fragrance was fading, replaced by Natalia's subtler scent. Within a few weeks of their meeting, that fragrance had permeated everything in his life—his apartment, his clothes, his truck, his bed. He'd fallen asleep to it, awakened to it, come to associate it with the best time of his life.

And it had all been just a job to her.

"Poor Anna." After a moment, she cleared her throat. "I think it's safe."

"Aw, Nat, why would I ever trust your opinion on that? The biggest danger in my life—in my brother's life—has come from you."

Shame crossed her face, and her gaze lowered to somewhere around his throat. "I'm sorry about what happened to Joe."

"But it would have been okay if they hadn't mistaken him for me."

"That's not what I meant. I never wanted you dead."

He wanted to believe that—wanted to believe he couldn't have been so wrong. He was the skeptic, the cynic, the con artist. Reading people was one of the tools of his trade. He knew better than to trust a pretty face.

But he *had* been wrong, and Joe had the scars to prove it. His brother had almost died in his place. Twice.

"I didn't know who the Mulroneys were," she whispered. "I didn't know they intended to kill you. I trusted Patrick. I didn't have a clue."

"How could you not know? Everyone knows." But that wasn't true. A lot of people in Chicago believed the brothers were exactly what they appeared to be: honest, hardworking, churchgoing businessmen. The Feds had tried a long time to build a case against them and had spent a lot of money and effort gaining the cooperation of insiders like Josh—and keeping them alive long enough to testify.

Natalia had been new to Chicago, an easy mark for someone like Patrick. She wouldn't have known the truth to start, and by the time she might have begun hearing rumors, she was already in his debt. She'd liked him, been grateful to him. Hadn't wanted to believe anything bad about him.

Aw, hell, don't start making excuses for her. You were a job to her, nothing more.

Even if she'd been so much more to him.

Chapter 3

Natalia's voice was unsteady when she spoke again. "We should leave."

"And go where?"

She shrugged, her arm bumping Josh's. It was a mere brush, lasting a second or two, but it warmed her in ways neither her coat nor the building's heating system had managed. For her own safety, she pressed herself harder against the wall. "There are all-night restaurants."

"Yeah, and Davison and Leeves will be checking every one of them."

"We can go back to my apartment." Even as she made the suggestion, she knew it wasn't possible. They may have seen only Davison and Leeves, but no doubt now that Josh had actually been sighted other people were involved, either new hires or newly-arrived from elsewhere. At least one of them would be watching her apartment.

Josh's expression was chiding, as if he expected better from her. "Don't you think your landlady called the police when she heard that gunshot?"

Unexpectedly, a tiny smile slipped free. "Probably not. Mrs. Johnstone takes her hearing aids out before the evening news so she doesn't accidentally catch any headlines."

His mouth relaxed, too, not quite forming a smile but close. He was handsome enough when scowling, but when he smiled, dear God, he was devastating. In their months together, he'd smiled a lot. She'd never known anyone as perpetually good-natured as him; it had been part of his attraction. No matter what was going on, he'd always found a reason to laugh…until she'd taken that from him.

Forcing her attention back to the subject, she said, "We could leave town."

"Yeah? And how would we do that? Steal a car? You learn how to hot-wire an engine the same time you learned to pick locks?"

His sarcasm stung, but she forced it away. Picking locks had saved her life—had saved their lives tonight. She wouldn't apologize for that.

"We could call J—"

Josh had started to move out of the corner, but he swung back, his face hard, his eyes icy. "No. We don't call Joe or Liz or anyone else. This is our problem. No one else's."

But Joe would come. So would Liz. Hell, deputy marshal that she was, Liz would know better than anyone how to get them safely out of Augusta, so they could disappear again. Separately. Hiding and never seeing each other again as long as they lived.

Though Natalia had been living alone, hiding from someone or another, for ten years, now the prospect sounded incredibly bleak.

"We'll stay here until morning," Josh decided, stepping through the opening. "We'll get out before the employees start showing up."

Once he'd put some distance between them, she was able to breathe again, though each breath smelled of him. She followed him into the room, deliberately sitting by the overpowering cinnamon- and fir-scented candles, giving her olfactory senses a break from his tantalizing scent.

"I'm beat." He dragged his fingers through his hair, then so quickly she couldn't react, he reached into her jacket pocket and pulled out the pistol. He tucked it into his own pocket, then extended his hand. "Give me the money."

Slowly she blinked. "Excuse me?"

"The money. I've got the gun. I want the cash."

Did he plan to ditch her? To take her weapon and her stash and run off, leaving her to deal with Davison and Leeves? Would he do that to her—this man who'd told her he loved her? This liar, this con artist, this thief?

This man whom she'd betrayed?

She stared at him, and he stared back, his expression inscrutable, his hand stone-cold steady as he waited for her to obey. "I thought you relied on charm to rob your victims blind," she said quietly as she pulled the stack of bills from her right jeans pocket.

He laughed. "You? My victim? Yeah, right. Besides, I know you. Charm's a waste of my time and yours." He gestured. "The rest of it."

He'd charmed total strangers for far less than he was taking from her, but *she* wasn't worth the effort. She swallowed the hurt and dug out the second stash of cash.

He shoved the money into his jeans pocket, then stuck his hand out once more. "Now the knife."

Grudgingly she removed the sheath from her ankle and offered it. He slid it into an inside jacket pocket before circling to the broken-down couch against the wall. "I'm gonna take a nap. Don't make me come looking for you when I wake up." He lay down, turned on his right side so the money and weapons would be impossible to reclaim without disturbing him, closed his eyes and went to sleep. *Like turning off a switch,* she used to tease.

Surprise made her slump back in the chair. He wasn't abandoning her. He was taking the best steps he could to keep *her* from abandoning *him*. Sure, she could make her escape with nothing more than the clothes she wore—she'd done it before—but money made it easier and, under the circumstances, weapons were vital.

But she wouldn't leave him, not like this. Not when he was in danger. Not when he needed her, no matter how much he didn't want her.

After three hours, the chair grew uncomfortable, causing an ache in the small of her back and another in her butt. She stood, stretched and set off the singing reindeer before hastily shutting it down. She would bet every dime of her twenty-eight hundred that opening the door would bring him instantly alert, but he didn't even twitch at the burst of song.

"Hey. Josh." She went to the door, her fingers wrapped around the knob, pulling it open just an inch or two.

His voice was a low, husky murmur from the shadows. "Where you going?"

"To find a bathroom. Want to come?"

What little light there was gleamed on his hair as he rolled over, then slid to his feet. He was scowling, not an angry, can't-stand-the-sight-of-her look but more a cranky-tired scowl. "Yeah. Hell, why not?" He picked up the flashlight she'd left on the table, pushed past her into the hall and shined the light in both directions. The best bet seemed a recessed area to the left, wide enough for two doors and a drinking fountain.

They walked there in silence, Natalia going into the ladies' room, Josh turning into the men's. She took care of business, washed her hands and face, then replaced her glasses to stare at her reflection in the mirror. She was too thin, too pale, and the hair color and style were too much. Her eyes were too big, too shadowed.

She was too tired.

There was a sound in the hall—an off-key whistling—and she straightened, finger-combed her hair and went out to find Josh leaning against the opposite wall. He pushed away. "Want to have a look around before we return to the cave?"

With a nod, she turned to the right. "Always like to know where the exits are. Don't you?"

"It comes in handy." After a few steps, he said, "No way for a grown man to live, huh?"

"No," she murmured, though the comment surprised her. He'd never held an honest job in his life. Jobs were for suckers, he'd said. He'd often tried to talk her into quitting her own job, never understanding why it was important to her to earn her way.

When the corridor ended, they turned left and followed a shorter hall to the front, then turned again into a lobby, glassed in on three sides. A lone light above the reception desk cast shadows across industrial carpet and overstuffed chairs.

"Joe and Liz got married in September." Josh stopped well back from the windows and stared out at the street. Natalia did the same. There was little traffic, and the stoplight at the nearby intersection blinked a slow, steady yellow.

"He owes you for that. If you hadn't taken off, she wouldn't have come looking for you and they wouldn't have fallen in love."

"I don't know. If they were meant to be together, they would have met somehow."

Meant to be together. She'd let herself pretend that sometimes: that Patrick Mulroney and lies and threats had brought them together, but only because that had been fate's intent. She'd pretended that all her problems would magically disappear, that he would never know about her deceit and they would live Happily Ever After.

But real life had always intruded on her fantasies. A relationship based on lies could never succeed; instead of going away, her problems would bury her alive; if he managed to survive, Josh would never forgive her; there would be no Happily Ever After. Hadn't her mother told her that from the time she was five?

"She's pregnant," Josh said, still staring at the street.

A sharp ache struck Natalia. Jealousy? Odd, since she'd really never thought about having children. Not even Josh's. "Really. I can't imagine a better father than Joe."

He looked sharply at her. "You know he loves Liz more than anything."

"Uh-huh." She watched a police car pass and wondered if the officer preferred quiet nights or a nice little shoot-out to liven up the long hours, then realized that Josh was still staring at her. She met his gaze. "I knew they were in love before they did." She'd helped save their lives, only a small part of the debt she owed the entire Saldana family. "Is Liz still with the marshals service?"

"No. She's working with Joe at the coffee shop until the baby's born. Then…" He shrugged.

Those last few weeks in Chicago, after he'd made the secret deal with the U.S. Attorney's office, Natalia had known something was up. Suddenly he'd had little time for her, making excuses about seeing a brother she hadn't known existed. At first she'd convinced herself that he was just working a particularly complex scam, but then she'd seen him with the woman she'd later learned was Liz. It had been a scam, all right. Just not the kind she'd expected—but exactly the kind Patrick had expected.

Sticking to the shadows, they crossed the lobby and followed the hallway to its end. In a few moments, they were back at the break room after identifying the front doors, one side door and the rear door they'd entered. Josh gestured toward the couch. "You want to sleep?"

"I'm fine." She stopped in front of the pop machine, shoved her hand into her jacket pocket, then grimaced. "Twenty-eight hundred dollars in cash, and I don't have seventy-five cents for a Coke."

He reached into his own pocket and pulled out a handful of change. She carefully picked out three quarters, doing her best not to touch the warm, callused skin of his palm, but her best wasn't enough. In search of an elusive coin, her nail scraped across his hand, and his skin twitched a tiny bit.

"You want anything?" She croaked like a frog, and immediately cleared her throat.

"Yeah, a Coke." He picked out three more quarters, dropped

them in her hand, then went to sit at one end of the couch. He waited until the machine spit out two cans and she'd brought one to him, then taken a seat at the opposite end to speak.

"When did you know you were setting me up for your buddy Patrick to kill?"

Josh watched her deliberate movements as she slid a rounded nail under the ring and popped it. Fizz escaped into the air, but she didn't take a drink right away. Instead she looked at him.

"When I heard about the shooting on the news. They didn't give Joe's name at first, but they had footage from the scene. I recognized your apartment building, your truck, and I couldn't find you. I kept calling your cell, your friends, the places where you hung out and Patrick. It was the next night when he and his brother came to see me. They were furious because I hadn't told them you had a twin brother."

He'd never told anyone about Joe. It was easy enough to hide; they didn't live in the same part of the city, frequent the same restaurants or clubs or run with the same people. The only times their lives had intersected had been at their parents' house in the 'burbs or when they got together for occasional—private—catch-up dinners.

Mostly it had been a lack of common interests. Twins or not, he and Joe hadn't been close since they were kids. Partly it had been for Joe's sake. His brother had been a hotshot investment guy who made fortunes for his clients and himself. Who would have trusted him with their money if they'd known his brother was a con artist?

And there had been one more reason for keeping Joe's existence from Natalia: jealousy. She'd been so damn beautiful and sexy and sweet. Why in hell would she have wanted him if she could have had his law-abiding, respectable, rich brother?

"I didn't believe Patrick," she went on, her voice barely audible. "I went to the hospital and I saw you leaving with Liz. Patrick filled me in on all the details then—what he did, what you'd done, what I'd done."

Josh fixed his gaze on a somewhat demonic-looking Santa, its glass eyes glowing in the dark. "Why didn't you leave?"

"I tried. But I had nowhere to go, and Sean said…well, it made sense to stay and continue working for them."

What had the bastard threatened her with? No doubt, her involvement in Joe's shooting. The Mulroneys knew who'd pulled the trigger; they'd had access to the gun. They would have had no qualms about sacrificing the shooter to punish Natalia.

He hoped the threat of being framed for attempted murder was the only lesson she'd needed.

"Patrick decided I needed closer supervision, so he put me to work in his office, and he kept me paired with people who taught me the ins and outs of working for them."

"You become an enforcer," Josh said, a laugh choking free. "Goody Two-shoes working as muscle for organized crime."

"I wasn't—"

Was she going to protest the Goody Two-shoes or the muscle comment? It didn't matter. Both were true, just like the *worthless* label Joe had hung on Josh when they were kids was true.

"My job was watching people, sometimes finding them, occasionally intimidating them." Pink tinged her cheeks as she talked. "I wasn't a Goody Two-shoes."

Josh stretched his feet out on a nearby chair. "I got into the business young—"

"Yeah, stealing your first car when you were five."

Little brother had been telling stories. He frowned at her, though there was no real annoyance behind it. "I know people. That's part of my job. And I know that you're no more cut out for this sort of thing than—than your landlady who doesn't want to hear anything bad on the news. You may have the mind for it, but not the heart. Inside, you're a good person."

Stubbornly she shook her head. "A good person wouldn't have gotten indebted to Patrick Mulroney. A good person would have gone to the police as soon as she figured out what was going on. A good person understands that's there something wrong about spying on people, about pretending to be something you're not."

That was one of the big differences between them: he was able to accept and blow off the things he'd done. Oh, he had a strong sense of right and wrong; his parents and Joe had seen to that. But when it interfered with what he wanted for himself, it was easy enough to ignore. Natalia, though, beat herself up over it. She was convinced she was going to hell for her sins. He probably was, too, but he preferred to enjoy the journey.

Abruptly he changed the subject. "Is there an all-night drugstore around here?"

She blinked. "Yeah, two or three blocks to the west. Do you need something?"

"If we're going to be out and about tomorrow, I need to do something about the way I look. Cut my hair, color it, shave…"

Immediately she slid forward. "You stay here and I'll—"

His smile was thin and chiding. "Right." He drained the last of his pop, threw the can into the trash, then pulled the pistol from his pocket. "I'm guessing you know how to use this."

Dislike flickered through her gaze, but she nodded.

"Well, I don't. The only time I've ever even held a gun was when I took one away from a sleeping marshal who was supposed to be watching me. The way he was slumped over, I didn't want it to fall and go off."

Her mouth twitched as if she wanted to laugh but didn't dare. Yeah, he'd been a big, bad guy, guarded twenty-four/seven by four deputy marshals. He hadn't even taken the pistol with him when he ran. He'd left it on the dining table.

"That was when you escaped." She pocketed the weapon, slung the duffel over her shoulder and around her neck, then led the way down the hall to the rear entrance. "Where did you go?"

"Everywhere. Nowhere. I laid low for a long time. Never slept the same place two nights in a row." Miserable months. Even the marshals had been better company than he'd found in himself. That was when he'd started thinking there had to be a better life out there. He wasn't stupid, just a little lax in morals. He could hold a regular job for a regular wage. He could live in the same town and go home to the same house every day. And if he could have a job and a house and a little self-respect, maybe someday—just maybe, he'd thought—he could have a family.

Maybe—he watched Natalia's long, easy steps and the sway of her hips as he followed—*they* could have a family. Or maybe not.

She unlocked the door, easing it open. The parking lot was silent, everything still. She eased out, then gestured to him. Lamps buzzed and a dog in a nearby backyard barked halfheartedly as they circled the building to the street out front. She turned right, and he fell into step beside her.

He pulled his jacket tighter. He'd never lived in the South before, but he was pretty damn sure it wasn't supposed to be this cold. Halos formed around the streetlights, probably ice crystals, because he was already losing contact with his toes.

"They're saying it might snow for Christmas," Natalia commented.

"If I'd wanted snow, I'd've gone to Chicago. Jeez, I hate the cold."

"So why aren't you on a beach in Mexico?"

He gave her a wry look. "Because the U.S. has an extradition treaty with them?"

"So *if* you got caught, they'd bring you back and turn you over to the marshals again." Her shrug said what she left unspoken: *Big deal.*

"And either I'd have to testify against the Mulroneys or I'd face charges myself. Either way, odds are I'd end up dead. No, thanks."

"You can't run forever."

"No, but I can do my own version of witness relocation. I can get my own documentation, and I can settle down someplace where no one would ever look for me. Besides—" he glanced both directions before stepping off the curb "—you aren't in Mexico. Going there wouldn't have helped me find you at all."

She ducked her head but didn't respond to that.

The neon lights of a chain drugstore brightened the night halfway down the block. The parking lot was empty except for a police car backed into an outside space. It was empty, too. Great.

A blast of heat greeted them as they went through the double doors. The cop was standing at the cash register, hands in his pockets, a big ugly gun on his hip. The clerk greeted them, and the cop gave them a once-over and a nod before returning to his conversation.

Natalia headed straight to the hair color halfway down the first aisle, scanning the boxes and quickly selecting a nice, plain brown. Next they got shaving stuff, a cheap bath towel and a pair of scissors, and he grabbed a couple of hoodies on the way to the checkout.

Cops made him antsy—had for as long as he could remember. Of course, he'd had his first run-in with them when he was five. That had been enough to put him off the entire profession for the rest of his life.

"How you doing?" the cop asked as they unloaded their purchases on the counter.

Natalia stiffened, making Josh's grin broader than he'd intended. "We're freezing our asses off. How about you?"

"Yeah, this weather is something. My kids are all excited about the chance of snow, but me, I'll take warm weather any time."

"I'm with you, buddy." He pulled out two twenties and handed them to the clerk, then pocketed the change. "Stay warm. And Merry Christmas."

"Yeah, you, too."

Picking up the bags in one hand, he steered Natalia toward the door with the other. As soon as they reached the far side of the parking lot again, tension rushed from her body, leaving her soft and warm beneath his palm.

"I hate cops," she murmured.

"One of the side effects of the life you've chosen."

She stepped away from his touch, then did something so rare in all the time he'd known her that his feet stopped moving: She told him something personal. "My father was a cop."

It took him only a second to get his feet working again, quickly enough that he doubted she'd even noticed his hesitation. In their time together, she'd told him exactly three things about her family: the bit about her grandmother, that she had two sisters and that she hadn't seen them in a long time. He didn't even know where she came from.

He couldn't think what to say. His first impulse was to pounce on it, to ask as many questions as he could get out while her confiding mood lasted. Since he knew it wouldn't last, all he managed was a mildly curious, "Where?"

She shoved her hair back, making him wish it was the short, pale brown he was accustomed to. *Hardly enough to run my fingers through,* he'd teased while he did just that. It was soft and fine as silk and he'd liked stroking it while she had stroked—

Oh, man.

"Florida," she said at last. "Orlando."

Wow. She was being damn near chatty. "I've always wondered…do families who live in Orlando go to Disney World or is that strictly a tourist thing?"

"Not our family." Her voice was as flat as her expression was fierce. Did she miss them that much? Or had they been that bad of a nightmare?

"What were they like?"

She kicked a piece of gravel and sent it skittering into the street. "The usual—Mom, Dad, his girlfriend, their two illegitimate daughters and me."

"Cozy. Mom and the girlfriend didn't object to each other?"

"Mom did. They fought about it a lot. Then he'd hit her and she'd let it drop…until the last time. She said if he wanted Traci that much, she'd get out of his way, and she took a fistful of pills with a bottle of rum. He moved Traci and their daughters in the day of the funeral." A long pause. "I was eight."

She said… "You were with her?" Josh couldn't keep the shock from his voice. No eight-year-old child should have to see her mother die. It was beyond cruel.

"I couldn't call 911 because he'd broken the phone when they were fighting, and I couldn't go to the neighbor's house because he'd locked us in."

Her sigh was so heavy and icy that he half expected to hear it shatter when it hit the pavement. How long had she been alone with her dead mother before the bastard had come back home? Had he given a damn about the trauma his little girl had gone through? Had he been the least bit sorry?

One look at Natalia, so stiff and self-contained, answered that.

Jesus.

As he tried to think of something worth saying, they approached the final street before their office building. A tire store sat on the corner, closed up tight. Heaps of old tires stood beside the building beneath a faded sign: *Recycle tires here*. That would make his environmentally-conscious brother happy.

"Listen, Nat—"

"Crap." Grabbing his arm, she yanked him toward the tires so hard that he damn near sprained an ankle. He followed her into the tiniest space she could find, burrowing like rats into a hole, and waited, barely breathing, for an explanation.

It came a moment later in the rumble of a heavy engine cruising up the street. They watched through cracks between tires as a black SUV came into sight. It was moving well below the speed limit, and despite the cold, the deeply-tinted windows were rolled down, giving them a good view of Mickey Davison in the passenger seat. His thick head was moving constantly, scanning from side to side, and his mouth was running, as it usually was.

His lungs giving out completely, Josh watched until they drove from sight, then sat down on his butt and exhaled. "Jeez, I'm too old for this shit."

Chapter 4

Natalia sat down beside him, ignoring the cold that instantly seeped into her jeans. Their space was so tight that her knees were bent practically to her chest, and all she could smell if she looked to the left was rubber.

To the right, it was Josh. His cologne was clean, citrusy, summery, and *he* smelled of danger. Enticement. The promise of pure pleasure.

Why had she told him so much about her family? He didn't care. He couldn't. He hadn't even said *I'm sorry,* though to be fair, he hadn't had much chance. But even back then, most people hadn't known what to say.

Her father hadn't had trouble. *Good riddance. I was tired of her, anyway.*

Neither had Traci. *Too bad the bitch didn't take her brat with her.*

Josh's breathing slowed. "You think they've been driving around all night looking for us?"

"I guess. After getting their tires fixed."

"Wonder if they did it here."

She glanced at the tires that provided them protection, imagining two bearing cuts from her knife, and from somewhere deep inside a laugh escaped.

Josh began chuckling, too. "Don't you know the Mulroneys are pissed at them? Having us cornered, then losing us?"

Her laughter slowly faded. The brothers were damn scary when things weren't going their way, and for a long time now, fate had been smiling the other way. *Find them,* they'd probably ordered Davison and Leeves, *or we'll find you.* And there was no doubt what would happen when they did.

"I bet they're regretting the day they met you."

"Are you?" He turned to meet her gaze, his expression gone serious. He was closer than she'd realized. If she leaned forward *this* much…but it was an impossible distance to cover.

"Are you regretting the day we met, Nat?"

She tried to look away. Tried to lie. But her mouth didn't care what her brain wanted. Her heart didn't care. "No," she whispered. "The circumstances, yes, but meeting you? Never."

Turned out, the distance wasn't so impossible. All she had to do was lean, just a tiny bit. He met her more than halfway, removing her glasses, gripping a handful of her jacket, pulling her the rest of the way. His skin was cold, his mouth undeniably hot as he coaxed her lips open, then slid his tongue inside.

It was astonishing how such simple—such intimate—contact could push everything else out of her mind. The cold, the fear, the alertness she lived with…all forgotten. Meaningless. For the moment only this kiss mattered, this touch, this sweet reminder of what she'd lost.

After a time he pulled back, and for one aching second, she followed him, clinging. With a rush of shame, she caught herself and would have crawled even deeper into the tires if he hadn't held onto her jacket like a lifeline. He stared at her, at a loss for words—probably a first for the slick, sweet-talking con man.

"What's wrong, Josh?" she asked, sliding her glasses on to better see his reaction. "Cat got your tongue?"

He blinked, and his fingers slowly unfolded from her jacket. "You always did remind me of a cat. Sleek. Powerful. Sexy."

It was her turn to blink. If she'd had to describe herself as an animal, she would have picked a mouse: small, drab, easy to overlook.

Or a rat.

Uneasily she shifted. "Do you think it's safe to go back to the cave?"

He let the intimacy fade as he shrugged his everyday, normal shrug. "We sure as hell can't stay here. Even if we shared our body heat, I'd freeze to death before the sun came up."

He got to his feet, then gave her a hand up. She took it, wishing she'd removed her gloves, wanting the feel of bare skin against skin.

Not that it lasted long. Once they'd cleared the maze of tires, he released her hand as they walked behind the garage, keeping to its shadows, then jogged to the back door of their building. Once again she picked the lock, and they returned to the break room.

Josh stripped off his jacket, ripped open the hair color package, then held out the scissors. "There's a ten-dollar tip in it if you don't make me look like a whack job."

Slowly she peeled off her gloves and her own jacket. "You're trusting me with scissors?"

"Honey, you've already got a gun. You don't need scissors to mess me up." He laid them in her palm, then muttered something under his breath as he swung a plastic chair around to sit on.

It sounded an awful lot like, *You did that all by yourself.*

Lacking a comb, she brushed his hair into order with her fingers, counseling herself silently. It wasn't sexy, it wasn't sensuous, it wasn't intimate. It was just a job. Thousands of stylists did it every day to both regular customers and strangers.

But she wasn't a stylist, and Josh wasn't a stranger, and she'd missed touching him, God, so much.

Her first cuts were conservative, taking off a fine spattering of blond hair. He looked at the floor, then snorted. "Give me the scissors."

When she did, he grabbed a thick hank of hair and blindly cut it near the roots before handing the scissors back. "Now cut the rest of it to match."

Obeying, she soon had a broom-worthy pile of hair on the floor. The big cuts were done, leaving her with the finer work, when he spoke again.

"What was it like having two sisters suddenly move in with you?"

Her hand trembled, snipping where she didn't mean to, but it was on the back of his head. He'd never know.

Should she answer? Her old practice of keeping her secrets her own hadn't gotten her anything in the past. Just a man who'd said he'd loved her without knowing that she wasn't worth loving.

When what she needed was a man who could love her even knowing that.

"Just call me Cinderella," she replied once her hand—and her voice—steadied. "I wasn't exactly popular at home. I talked about my mom. I cried for her. I had nightmares about her. Traci preferred her own daughters, of course, and so did our father. They liked me best when I was locked in the utility room after I'd done my chores. That was where they'd moved me so her girls could have my room."

She smiled faintly. An aluminum cot, a washer, a dryer and the smell of bleach—that had meant home to her for a long time.

"Did you ever tell anyone?" Josh's tension knotted the muscles in his neck as well as his voice. It was sweet that he could be angry about something that had happened so long ago to a woman who'd betrayed him.

"I tried, but my timing sucked." She laughed rustily. "It was the day before Christmas break when I told my teacher. She took me to the counselor, and the counselor called a meeting with my father and Traci. They denied it, of course, and in the end, everyone agreed it was the trauma of my mother's death making me act out, and they took me home... I had two and a half weeks for the bruises to heal before school started again, and I never told anyone else until tonight. Until you."

He twisted his head to meet her gaze. There was so much in his expression: anger, impotence, sympathy, frustration. "Is your father still alive?"

"Last I heard."

"Hot-wire a car for us, and we can lead Davison and Leeves right to his door."

The small, terrified little girl that still cowered inside her smiled at the idea of unleashing the goons on her unsuspecting father. The woman who clung to that little girl, though, couldn't do more than contemplate such a thing. "I don't want him dead."

"Even after what he did to you? To your mother?"

She shook her head.

Josh rolled his eyes. "And you claim you're not a Goody Two-shoes."

He turned back so she could finish the haircut. The back and sides done, she moved in front of him to trim the bangs that fell across his forehead to brush his brows. He sat still, his eyelids fluttering shut as bits of hair drifted down onto his cheeks. She held her breath as she leaned close for a final inspection, then murmured, "All done."

He scrubbed his hand over his face before locking gazes with her again. "You really didn't know they were going to kill me, did you?"

She shook her head, and this time, she thought, he believed her.

He touched her face gently, brushing something away—a snip of hair, a speck of nothing—then stood and pulled a crumpled ten from his pocket. "Here's your tip."

"From my own money?" She stuffed the bill into her pocket. If they got separated, at least she wouldn't be flat broke.

"Hey, I had some cash on me when I showed up tonight. Not much, but some." A glance at the clock, and he amended that. "Last night. How long will this color take?"

"A half hour or so."

"Time to shave, too, and then we'd better be getting out of here."

"And go where?"

"It's your town. You choose."

She found a whisk broom and dustpan under the sink and cleaned up while he started the coloring process. Where could they go? It was Christmas Eve, freezing cold and there was an unknown number of killers looking for them.

Her first impulse was simple enough: the Feds. They would arrest her, and turn Josh over to the marshals, who would take him back to Chicago. Maybe she could make a deal with them, too; she knew enough about the Mulroneys' business, especially their activities in Georgia, where they'd ordered the kidnapping and murder of a deputy U.S. marshal, to be of some value to the U.S. Attorney's office.

Maybe she and Josh could go into witness protection together if they survived the trials.

The scent of chemicals stung her nose as she dumped the hair into the trash can. Christmas Eve should smell differently; there should be peppermint and cocoa, pecan pies baking, eggnog and fresh, hot bread. At least, that was what she remembered from the few Christmases before her mother died.

"What will your parents do for Christmas?"

Using vinyl gloves to smear goop into his hair, Josh glanced at her. If he felt melancholy or homesick, it didn't show. "Joe and Liz are driving down Christmas morning to spend a couple of days with them. On Sunday, they're flying to Kansas to visit her family, and Mom and Dad are going on a cruise."

"Nice." She'd never met the elder Saldanas, but Josh had always spoken of them affectionately. He'd had a perfectly normal upbringing, he'd told her, with perfectly normal parents. Now that she'd told him of her upbringing, did he have a better appreciation of *normal?*

He held up the color applicator bottle. "There's a lot of this left. Wanna get rid of that red?"

Thinking of how much she hated both the color and cut of

her hair, she eyed the bottle. "I thought all men were hot for redheads."

"Not all. Some of us like plain ol' brown. Sit."

After a moment, she did as he ordered, and he began working the solution into her hair. Her eyes stung and her nose got sniffly, but she didn't kid herself that it was from the chemicals. She'd been wrong earlier. Having him work on her hair *was* sexy, sensuous and intimate. By the time he finished, she wasn't sure whether she was a boneless mass waiting for him to do what he would or a bundle of raw nerves. Either way, she was wowed.

"Thanks," she murmured as he threw the gloves away.

He grinned the charm-her-socks-off grin. "You can tip me later."

She watched the clock while he shaved, then they took turns at the sink, shampooing their hair. After she towel-dried hers, she offered him the scissors. "Cut it, will you?"

He didn't hesitate. In moments, hunks of newly auburn hair littered the floor, and she felt ten pounds lighter. While she swept up, he pulled on a black hoodie, then his coat, and tossed the second hoodie on the table. "We'd better get out of here. Where are we going?"

Natalia's stomach knotted. The break room was the only place she felt safe. Once they set foot outside the building, every person they saw would be suspect. People would be looking for them, and not all of them looked the part of hired killer like Davison. Some of them would look quite innocent. Like her.

But staying here wasn't an option. People would begin coming in soon—if not to actually work, then for the Christmas party the woman last night had mentioned. She tugged the hoodie on, combed her hair back in place, then stuffed their other purchases into her duffel. Sacrificing a few minutes to trade her glasses for the contact lenses in her bag, she pulled on her coat and gloves before giving Josh a this-is-it look. "I think we should turn ourselves in."

"Yeah, that's funny."

"I'm serious. You'll be okay, just back with the marshals for a while. And I—I can work something out."

He propelled her down the hall and to the rear exit. "I don't *want* to be back with the marshals, and you don't want to 'work something out.' Trust me."

She dragged to a stop at the door. "What I don't want, Josh, is to hide the rest of my life."

"You think you won't be doing just that if you make a deal with the Feds? In less than two years, they had me in six states. I never got to go anywhere or do anything. The only time I was alone was in the bathroom and in bed. They drove me freaking crazy. If you want to be the government's prisoner, go ahead, but leave me out of it. I'm not going back."

She believed that he'd hated every minute of it…but she also believed it was better than dying. Shouldering him aside, sliding her hand inside her pocket to grip the pistol, she eased the door open, looked to the left, then stepped outside, flat against the building, and scanned to the right. Giving him the okay, she shrugged, pulled the hood over her damp hair and said, "At least there would be someone in my life."

Without giving him a chance to respond, she began walking with long strides toward the street. "Come on. We're taking a bus tour of Augusta."

She hadn't been kidding, Josh reflected hours later. They'd hopped from bus to bus, wandering aimlessly around the city. The local residents embraced the Christmas season with open arms. Every place they passed, business or home, bore decorations, and too often when the bus doors opened, carols drifted in from someplace nearby. If things were different—he glanced at Natalia—it could be nice. Hell, even joyous. But, jeez, it was hard to get in the Christmas spirit when people were trying to kill you.

"I'm starved."

"Me, too." Natalia, sitting beside the window with her back turned out, roused from her stupor. As far as he knew, she hadn't gotten any sleep last night, and it showed. She'd been semi-comatose since they'd transferred from the last bus.

She looked around, getting her bearings. "We're not far from the mall. We can go there."

He stared at her. "Are you kidding?"

"It's not the one I work at. It's Christmas Eve. It'll be crowded."

"They'll be watching it."

"Looking for a blond man with a beard and a red-haired woman. They'll have to look twice to recognize us, and there are plenty of exits."

He still thought it was a crappy idea, but when the bus slowed and she stood up, he stood, too, stepping into the aisle, allowing her to go ahead of him.

Traffic was at a crawl, both going into and coming out of the mall. Parking spaces were at a premium and, inside, so was walking space. God, he hoped no one took a shot at them, because in this kid- and stroller-choked environment, it would be tough to run, and who else might get hurt?

"Nat, I don't think this is a good idea."

Concern flickered across her face. "You're probably right. Let's get something to eat, then get out of here."

She headed straight to the food court, where they stood in line for grilled-chicken sandwiches. All the tables were full, so they found a bench nearby, each sitting at one end, leaving space between them for a table of sorts.

Once his first sandwich was gone, Josh took a bite of the second before voicing something that had been on his mind since they'd left the office building. "You don't have to live so alone, Nat. Joe and Liz know you saved their lives." When Josh had escaped the marshals' custody, the Mulroneys had figured, as the Feds had, that eventually he would turn to his brother for help, as he'd always done. The Feds had sent Liz to Copper Lake. The Mulroneys had sent Natalia. When Josh had failed to appear, the Mulroneys had tried to force Joe into giving up his location by kidnapping Liz. In saving their lives, Natalia had put her own in danger, and his brother and sister-in-law understood that. "They'd be happy to have you back in Copper Lake."

"Right. And when Patrick sends someone to find me, they could be in danger, too—or their baby." As if to demonstrate the conversation was closed in her opinion, she turned her back while she continued to eat.

Her sarcasm had been heavy, but underlying it was something else. Wistfulness. Whether she wanted to admit it, she'd gotten close to Joe and Liz; his brother had told him as much. She'd let them get closer than anyone besides Josh had ever gotten, and she missed them.

If the Mulroneys and their goons were in prison, there'd be no reason for anyone to go looking for her. She could live where she wanted, do what she wanted. *Be* wanted.

If they were in prison. And Josh could put them there.

But then *he* could never live where he wanted.

He was selfish and a coward, because he couldn't face going back into protective custody and then into relocation for the rest of his life. As he'd told her, he'd rather live his own version. A little danger seemed a fair trade-off for a whole lot of freedom.

Beside him, on the other side of a tall green plant, a group of teenage boys leaned against the railing. They talked about girls they were dating, gifts they were expecting, family dinners they were being forced to attend. Josh didn't have to wonder if he had been so self-absorbed when he was their age. Hell, he'd been like that at twice their age. But he was changing. He really was.

"Hey, look at that clown over there," one of them called, gesturing to a man on the other side of the mall. "He looks like he's trying to direct traffic for a bunch of morons."

Like the other boys, Josh's head swiveled around, and his gaze zeroed in on Clive Leeves, standing at the opposite railing, gesturing with both arms. Toward *them*.

Josh jerked back around, then tried to spot Leeves's accomplice in the crowd, but sitting down made that impossible and the instant he stood up…

"Nat, Leeves is here and he's seen us. Which way to the closest exit?"

Stunned, she spit the food in her mouth into a napkin. "It's at the food court. But that's away from the main street. We need to go back to the right."

"Okay. Look for anyone who looks out of place. Ready?" When she nodded, he took her arm and together they rose from the bench. He gave their rear a sweeping gaze as they eased into the flow of people and saw a face familiar from Chicago—skinny guy, always in a bad mood. A hundred feet ahead was another: Davison trying to muscle his way through the crowd toward them.

"Is that what you mean by looking out of place?" Natalia asked dryly.

"He fits the description for me. What do you think, Nat? I've always been on the nonviolent side of the business. The last time I hit someone was when Brent Jacobi and I fought over Melissa Cardone in eighth grade, and I broke my hand." He grinned ruefully. "Turned out she didn't like either of us. She was after Joe."

Her smile was faint, but reassuring. "Work your way to the left, but stay with that bunch of girls. When I give you the signal, run like hell. The door's just past the sporting goods place."

"What signal?" he asked as she moved behind him, out of his sight.

"You'll know it when you hear it."

That didn't sound good. Josh increased his pace, pushing past people to get behind a dozen teenage girls who didn't seem to be shopping for anything more than pricey coffee drinks. He didn't look back but felt the pressure of Natalia's hand holding onto his jacket.

Davison changed course to intersect with them before the exit, and the murmurs of irritation rising behind them suggested the skinny guy was moving in, too. Farther ahead, someone else was in a hurry, too, this guy a stranger, leaving disgruntled shoppers in his wake.

"Come on, Nat. Do something." At this rate, the clowns were going to grab them less than fifty feet from the door, and they'd have no choice but to go along.

And then they'd die.

A broad grin spread across Davison's face as he stopped a few yards away. Josh stopped, too, to avoid getting swept right into his arms.

"You won me a fifty-dollar bet, Saldana. Frank said that wasn't you. Said it was too clean-cut. But a shave and a haircut don't fool me. I've spent so much time looking for you that I've been seeing your ugly face in my dreams."

"Sorry, Mickey," Josh said easily, "but you're not my type."

Davison made an obscene gesture, then opened his coat to show the pistol he wore. "Don't make me—"

A piercing scream echoed through the mall, damn near bouncing off the rafters. "Oh, my God, that man in the Bears jacket has a gun!" Natalia shrieked. "Help, help, he has a *gun!*"

Panic erupted, people shouting, jostling, running. Mothers grabbed their children and rammed their strollers into anyone in their way. The girls they'd been following raced into the nearest store in hysterics. Everyone ran—to them, away from them, it didn't seem to matter.

"Freeze!" a police officer yelled, and Natalia gave Josh a shove from behind. Giving Davison a wink, he grabbed her hand, and they joined the stampede of shoppers heading for the door.

The cold hit like a shock wave. People gathered in knots in the parking lot, traffic was snarled, and sirens wailed. When he slowed to a walk, Natalia pulled at him. "They only got Davison. The rest will be after us. Come on."

They ran to the end of the building, then started across the parking lot, dodging cars trying to leave. When tires squealed behind them, Josh risked a second to look just in time to see Leeves sighting in on them over the roof of the SUV.

"Oh, jeez." For the first time, instead of following, Josh

took the lead, finding the energy in adrenaline, dragging Natalia with him and diving behind the cover of a Dumpster a split second before Leeves fired. Instantly they were up and running again, keeping obstacles between them and the SUV. He counted three—no, four more shots before they reached the congestion of the street.

They turned east on the easier path of the sidewalk, though they couldn't stay in the open for long. Either Leeves would leave the truck and come after them on foot, or he would send his people after them. They had to disappear first.

"Cab," Natalia called, and he saw it sitting at a red light ahead. The windows were rolled up and the driver was singing along with the stereo. If the light changed before they got to the intersection—

Like the scream in the mall that had set off a thousand heart attacks, the whistle she gave could have pierced eardrums. It penetrated the closed windows and the music, making the cabbie turn their way. He cracked the window and grinned. "Want a ride?"

Josh jerked open the back door, gave Natalia half a second to slide inside before he dove in practically on top of her. "Man, I'm really too old for this shit."

Chapter 5

"Drive toward downtown," Natalia instructed as she pulled the duffel's strap over her head. "But take the long way. Through the residential areas." She started to slide across the seat, but Josh caught her hand, holding her where she was. Tension of a new kind streaked through her, making her heart stutter and her muscles go weak.

His cheeks were ruddy from the cold, his eyes bright with hyperalertness. When he eased his grip a bit, his hand shook, and his breathing was slow to return to normal. He looked... incredible.

"You kids all ready for Christmas?" the driver asked.

"As ready as we'll ever be. How about you?"

"Nah, that's my wife's department. She's been shopping since June. We've got six kids and seventeen grandkids. It takes a long time. So...you just killing time before all the fun starts?"

"Yeah. It's his first time in Augusta. I thought we'd give him plenty to see." With a deep breath—casual conversation was *so* not her strong suit—she leaned back, resting her head against the seat, closing her eyes.

She was breathing slowly—the scent of Josh, hair-color chemicals, taxicab smells—when something different caught her attention. It was faint until she rolled her head to the left and concentrated. She knew the smell—it was one of those you never forgot—and it was coming from Josh. From his hoodie, to be exact.

Setting the duffel on the seat next to the door, she twisted to face him, lifting the black hood where it hung down his back. She ran her fingers over the fabric and swallowed hard when her index finger slid neatly through a hole on one side of the hood and out another on the opposite side. The pounding of her heart made her breath catch audibly, and he turned a concerned look on her. Following her stare, he twisted to look over his shoulder, then grabbed the hood and stretched it around so he could see.

His face paled. She was sure she'd gone even whiter.

One of Leeves's shots had torn right through the hood, an inch, no more than two, from Josh's head, leaving behind ragged fabric and the smell of gunpowder. With the high-powered ammunition Leeves preferred, just a few millimeters to the right, and likely no wound would have been survivable.

Josh had almost been killed.

Grabbing the sides of his jacket, she yanked him forward and pressed her mouth to his. It was a fierce kiss, filled with fear and anger and wanting and needing. Dear God, if he'd been hit, if he'd died, what reason would there be for her to go on?

If her ferocity stunned him at first, soon enough he'd recovered. He slid his arms around her, pulling her as near as he could in the cramped seat, and kissed her back with just as much fear and anger and wanting. His hands slipped beneath her jacket, roaming restlessly, tugging at her shirt, seeking bare skin. She shuddered and made a soft little whimper, swallowed by his mouth.

"Where are you fro—" The driver chuckled. "It's hard when

you're staying with your folks and can't get any privacy, isn't it? Never mind me. I'll keep my eyes forward and my mouth shut."

Barely able to make sense of his words, Natalia laid her palms against Josh's cheeks. It had been nearly three years since she'd touched him, but her hands remembered the feel of him. Her skin *knew* him; her fingers delighted in the shape and the touch of him. Her hands, her mouth, her whole body, knew this was *home*.

Desperate for air, she drew back just enough to break the kiss. Their noses still bumped, and his strangled breathing warmed her lips. His eyes darkened to a stormy blue, he whispered, "Did you believe I loved you?"

She was halfway through a shake of her head when it became a nod. She'd been afraid to believe it—afraid that her father was right and she wasn't worth it, that he'd disappear and break her heart. But somewhere deep inside she'd believed enough to love him back.

"That's why I did it," he continued to whisper, the words little more than a brush of air between them. "Why I made the deal with the Feds. I wanted a chance to be normal. I wanted to be better than I was, to have something to offer you." His expression turned abashed. "To stay out of prison, too, but to have a reason to stay out. To straighten up and be someone you could be proud of."

"I would have run away with you at any time."

"I didn't know that. I didn't know…"

A lot of things. That she was no better than the life he'd wanted to leave behind. That she was more a liar than he'd ever been. That *she* wasn't someone *he* could be proud of.

The hope and heat and pleasure generated by their kiss deflated, sinking heavily in her stomach. "And finding out changed everything."

He gazed past her for a time before giving her a raised-brows look that substituted for a shrug. "I make a lot of bad decisions, Nat."

The lump in her stomach turned to ice as she carefully

disengaged from him and sat back. Which was his latest bad decision? Kissing her? Admitting that he'd loved her? Tracking her down in the first place?

He let her go, but not her hand. His fingers gripped hers firmly, holding it on his knee. His head turned away from her, staring out the window, he quietly asked, "Where were you before Chicago?" No need for such intimate whispers now.

Speaking required a deep breath and more effort than she'd expected. "I ran away from home when I was fifteen and wound up in Jacksonville. I hadn't had any contact with the family for years when I started getting letters from my youngest half sister. She had located me somehow, and she wanted to…to be sisters."

There'd been no possibility of that when she'd lived at home; Traci had encouraged both girls to treat Natalia the same way their parents did, and the older one had delighted in it. Allie had tried to be friendly, but after seeing Natalia punished for it, she'd taken to ignoring her completely.

"Our father found out, and he threatened me. He never made idle threats, so I left town the next day. Chicago was as far as I could go on the money I had."

Josh looked at her. "And there you met Patrick. Then me. You ever notice how fate has a way of screwing with some people?"

Her own look was dry enough to rattle. "Fate, destiny, fortune…my whole life has been a cluster—"

"Nat! Goody Two-shoes don't say that word."

She primly closed her mouth, waited a beat, then murmured, "I've said it before."

"Not to me. And you never can—" he leaned closer and his voice dropped to a husky, make-her-blood-pump shiver "—unless we're both naked and have a *lot* of time to pass." He followed the words with a wink and an impossibly sexy grin before settling back to watch the scenery again.

Both naked. Her heart was beating wildly again. He was entertaining the possibility that they could have wild, wicked sex at least once more. Just the idea made her throat dry and her stomach flip-flop. She had resigned herself to living the rest of her life the way she'd spent the past few years—celibate—but a few kisses, a few words and a wink, and she was ready to strip down then and there.

Even if it was his latest bad decision.

Even if it meant getting her heart broken all over again.

Even if this time she might not recover.

She scoffed. She hadn't recovered the last time. She'd lived like a robot—doing the jobs the Mulroneys demanded of her, too defeated to run again, too hopeless to care. The closest she'd come to really living had been her weeks in Copper Lake, with Joe and, later, Liz. Even though, their biggest value to her had been the constant reminders of Josh. She'd just existed, and, after fleeing there to avoid arrest, she'd hardly done even that.

From the last time she'd seen Josh in Chicago to the moment she'd recognized him in the yard last evening, she'd barely been getting by.

There should be more to life than barely getting by.

Traffic got lighter as they neared downtown. Most businesses had closed early for Christmas Eve, their employees gone to the malls for shopping or home to prepare for the festivities. The cabdriver would be wanting to head that way soon to get in as much time as he could with his six kids and seventeen grandkids. She and Josh needed a plan, and the only one coming to mind was the one he'd rejected: turning themselves in. It was rational. Sane. Relatively safe.

But would he ever forgive her for betraying him a second time?

They were stopped at a red light when she saw a fast-food restaurant ahead, its neon light flashing *Open.* Her stomach clenching, she looked at Josh, mouthed, *Bathroom break,* then leaned over the seat. "Excuse me, sir, could you pull in there just for a minute?"

The driver grinned. "It's your meter, hon. You can take as long as you want."

When Josh started to open the passenger door, she stopped him. "I'll be right back. Watch my bag, will you?"

Hesitation crossed his face, but finally he closed the door again. "If you need anything—"

"I'll fire three times in the air."

"Hell, don't waste the ammo."

She flashed him a smile before climbing out, hustling the few feet to the restaurant door and disappearing inside. It wasn't much warmer inside than out, leaving condensation thick on the windows. She got change from the counter girl, then did go to the bathroom—one of the few pieces of intelligent advice Mickey Davison had ever given her: *never miss a chance to take a leak.* But her real goal was the pay phone in the bathroom hallway.

Her hands trembled when she picked up the receiver and dropped in a coin. It took courage to dial the numbers, and she almost hung up with every ring. Josh would be furious with her for going against him, and even more so for involving others, but she had no idea where else to turn late on Christmas Eve afternoon.

"Hi, you've reached Liz at A Cuppa Joe. Merry Christmas, and why aren't you here at the shop celebrating our first and hereafter annual Christmas Eve coffee klatch?"

Natalia wasn't sure whether the faint feeling came from hunger, dread, stress or simply hearing Liz's voice again, all bright and happy, but she braced herself against the wall. "Hey, Liz. It's Natalia. I—I need your help."

Josh didn't realize he was holding his breath until the glass door swung open and Natalia came out. She looked fine, unharmed, beautiful and troubled—and that last part came from him. He was tired of putting those expressions on the faces of people he loved.

"I guess our tour's lasted long enough," she announced, giving the driver an address.

Josh wondered where they were going, but in minutes they

were at their destination: a waterfront park called Riverwalk. He paid off the cabbie, traded Christmas well-wishes with him, then shouldered the duffel as the car drove away. "This is it?"

"No, we're headed a few blocks away. But this is my favorite place in Augusta. I come here on pretty days. I just want to see it…"

One last time? Before something happened, before she had to flee again?

She took his hand and they walked past the statue of James Oglethorpe and through an opening in the levee. The Savannah River looked dark and cold. His parents were a couple hours down that river, but he'd never felt farther from them.

Natalia didn't linger long staring at the river. After a moment, she gazed around the early winter darkness with a shiver, then smiled tautly. "We should go."

It took a few minutes of brisk walking to reach a squat, square building. In earlier days, it might have been a department or furniture store, but now it was home to a shelter. He gazed in the plate-glass windows and saw bright lights, Christmas decorations, lots of tables and chairs and people milling about. Most of them looked happy to have someplace to be on Christmas Eve, out of the cold and with the promise of a hot meal.

They were greeted by a shelter worker, given cups of cocoa and directed to tables laid out with Christmas cookies, snacks, cheeses and breads. From the kitchen at the back came the aromas of dinner cooking.

"Nice spread," he commented.

"People donate a lot of food at Thanksgiving and Christmas. The holiday spirit, you know." Natalia didn't sound as cynical as he thought she might have twenty-four hours earlier.

Most of the chairs and sofas were occupied, so they found a table they could lean against near a large central pillar and still see most of the large room. Josh located an exit on the south side of the building and a sign indicating another at the rear on the north side. *Always like to know where the exits are, don't you?* Damn straight.

Not a way for a grown man to live, huh?

Damn straight.

In the center of the room stood a Christmas tree, decorated with twinkling lights and glass balls. Children sat beside it with their parents, young couples held hands and gazed at it longingly, and old men stared sightlessly at it, probably lost in memories of better times, happier Christmases.

He didn't want another homeless-shelter Christmas in his future—or Natalia's. You could run from your problems for only so long. Even if they didn't catch up with you, there was always the fear that they would, and that was no way to live. It was no way to ask someone else to live.

But testifying against the Mulroneys, probably having to be relocated with a new identity, leaving his parents and his brother behind for the rest of his life…

Or refusing to testify, going to trial and hoping that the Mulroneys didn't have someone in the system kill him to send a message. Asking Natalia to wait five or ten years on the off chance that he did survive, hoping that his enemies didn't take their revenge on her…

He sighed heavily, and she looked at him. "What?"

"I hate it when the only choices are crappy, crappier and crappiest."

Her pretty features screwed into a frown, but before she could ask when he meant, movement near the main entrance caught his attention. Two men had just come through the door, and three more waited outside at the curb where a van sat. The cost of Clive Leeves's suit would have fed the shelter's clients for a month or two, and some of them recognized that as they eyed him speculatively. They paid little attention to skinny, cranky Frank at his side.

It looked as if Josh had just been given one more option: very likely die in the next few minutes.

As the men scanned the room, he eased closer to Natalia.

momentarily blocked from their view by the massive column. "Take this, would you?" Reaching into his left pocket, he pulled out the wad of cash and surreptitiously pressed it into her palm, then did the same with the second wad.

She stared at it. "You're giving it back?"

He grinned. "It's your money. Besides, what're you going to do now that you've got it? Run out on me?"

Her green gaze was solemn, intent. "You know I wouldn't."

"I know." He swallowed hard and hoped she would forgive him for running out on her. Tugging the hood up to cover her hair, he forced another grin. "Go to the john. Fix it so you don't have lumps in your pockets. You don't want to tempt anyone in here to find out what they are."

She hesitated a moment, and he wondered where Leeves and Frank were in the large room and how long it would take one of them to spot him. Then, with a shrug, she pushed away from the column and headed to the hallway under the Restrooms sign.

Barely breathing, Josh watched until she was out of sight, then looked around. Leeves was at one end, checking out everyone gathered around the food, and Frank was at the other, slowly circling every sitting area and clump of people. Hands shoved in his pockets, shoulders hunched and head down, Josh started toward the door on the north side. His heart was thudding, his palms beginning to sweat. He deliberately wove around people where Leeves would have a clear view of him if he only looked up.

After a moment, Leeves did just that and slowly smiled. He shifted his overcoat enough that Josh could see the weapon underneath. As if Josh would be stupid enough to think him unarmed. The bastard always carried at least two guns, and so did skinny Frank—guns that could do a tremendous amount of damage in the crowded shelter.

Josh acknowledged Leeves with a slight nod, taking his

hands from his pockets, holding them out loosely at his sides in a sign of surrender.

Leeves spoke into his cell phone as he made his way to Josh's side. "Smart choice, Saldana. It would have ruined a lot of people's holiday if you'd tried to run."

"I'm tired of running."

"Where's Natalia?"

Good. They hadn't seen her. "We parted ways. Funny thing—she didn't like getting shot at because of me."

"She's good at saving her own skin, isn't she?" Leeves gestured as Frank joined them, and together they hustled Josh out the north door, where the van waited. They shoved Josh into the back, doors slammed, and before Josh had recovered from hitting the hard metal floor, they were moving.

He sat up, rubbing a sore spot on his shoulder. "How'd you find me?"

"We've got people spread all over this city."

Josh grinned. "You got lucky, huh?" And here *he* was always known as the lucky one. Well, luck had to run out sometime, didn't it? "Are we going back to Chicago? Because if we are, I need some warmer clothes. Even though it's Christmas Eve, I imagine we can find a store that's open where I can get a coat and gloves."

Frank spoke for the first time. "You don't need them where you're going." To the driver, he said, "This is good. Let us out here."

Josh looked around, but there were no windows in the rear of the van and one of Leeves's thugs blocked the view out the windshield. They'd driven only a few minutes, so they must still be in downtown Augusta. Then the back door swung open, and he smelled damp and saw the breach in the levee.

Riverwalk. He was going to die on Christmas Eve at Natalia's favorite place in Augusta, and if his body didn't get tangled in branches along the way, it would float right on down to Savannah, past his parents' new hometown.

Jeez, what was worse than crappiest?

His soon-to-be-ended life.

But at least Natalia had a chance to get away. And she knew he'd loved her. And though she'd never said the words, he knew she loved him, too.

It wasn't much, but it had to be enough.

Chapter 6

Oh, God.

Natalia stood rooted in place, staring across the room to the north side where the van had driven away moments earlier. Leeves had found them, and damn it, Josh had known. That was why he'd given her the money, why he'd sent her to the bathroom, so he could convince Leeves that she wasn't with him.

So he could save her life.

Now she had to find a way to save his.

Her gaze darted around the room. Liz had directed her to find shelter, had told her that someone—local police or federal—would meet them there to take them into protective custody. Where the hell was a cop when you needed one?

"Natalia Parker?"

Eyes wide with shock, she spun around and found herself facing three somber men. Though they were dressed casually in khakis and jeans, she would have made them for Feds—pissed-off Feds, for having their Christmas Eve interrupted. "They've taken Josh!" she blurted out, pointing out the window where she'd seen the van pull away. Without waiting for their response, she raced toward the door.

She hardly noticed the chill or the duffel bumping against her as she ran. The van had made a left turn on the next street, disappearing from sight. As she continued her desperate search, voices came from behind her, muffled by other running feet, and a moment later an SUV passed.

"Natalia. *Natalia*." The man who'd spoken to her in the shelter grabbed her arm, yanking her to a stop. "They'll keep them in sight."

She twisted to free herself, but his grip didn't lessen. "Let me go. I've got to—got to—"

"Got to what?"

Save Josh. She stared after the two vehicles, giving up her struggle as cold seeped way down inside her. *Or die trying*.

"We've got guys on them," the man said. "The brothers, too."

Her head whipped around. "The Mulroneys are here?"

"Flew in this afternoon. Apparently, they want to make sure the job gets done this time." Realizing that "the job" meant killing the man she loved, he grimaced. "By the way, I'm Deputy Marshal Kramer."

She turned back to stare down the street. All she could make out was two sets of brake lights, one some distance behind the other. Anxiously she tried to determine distances in the dark. And realized the van was stopped in the vicinity of Riverwalk. Quiet, deserted at this time of night, with the Savannah River to wash away all evidence of a murder.

Yanking free of Kramer, she began running again, darting into shadows where she could. She passed the SUV, now empty, and approached the van, also empty. Parked a short distance away was a black limo, its engine running, the driver gesturing while talking on a cell phone.

Natalia ducked into the shadows, scaled a low fence, then climbed to the top of the levee. The sight below was close to her worst nightmare: Josh, only a few feet from the river, hands raised; Leeves and Frank facing him, both pointing weapons;

Patrick and Sean Mulroney standing safely behind their thugs and three more men, strangers, guarding the entrance.

"You're just delaying the inevitable, Saldana," Patrick said, his voice carrying on the cold night air. "You're going to die here and now. It's up to you whether it's easy or hard. Where is Natalia?"

"I told your boys, I don't know. We split up after the incident at the mall." Josh sounded strong, his usual careless self, but she caught the hint of panic hidden in his expression. He expected to die, and he intended to do so protecting her.

"You spent all this time looking for her, and you let her walk away after less than twenty-four hours?"

Josh shrugged. "All I wanted from her was some answers. I got them."

"All you wanted was to spend the rest of your miserable life with her." Sean looked like his brother but sounded much harder. Crueler. *Was* much crueler. "Everyone knew you were—what'd you call it? Stupid in love with her. You tell us where she is, and Clive will kill you easy. You make us find her, you'll both suffer."

Natalia drew her pistol from her pocket. It was a nine millimeter, a good fit for her hand, with fourteen shots in the magazine and one more in the chamber. She was an excellent shot, but was that enough to save Josh's life? Josh had no cover but the frigid water. By the time she'd dropped the first two, one of the others would take aim on him.

"Parker!" The whisper came from behind her an instant before Deputy Marshal Kramer dropped to the ground beside her. Grasping her gun hand, he bent so his mouth was next to her ear. "We've got people in place. Just give us a distraction." As quickly as he'd appeared, he melted back into the shadows.

Natalia swallowed hard, returned the gun to her coat pocket, then crawled halfway down the hill. Standing, she drew a breath and said, "I don't know, Mr. Mulroney. I think other people have suffered enough for you. It's time to do your own suffering."

Seven heads swiveled in her direction. Josh took advantage of the moment to make a run for it, dashing across the pavement, crashing off into the trees. At the same time, Natalia dove, landing hard a dozen feet away, wriggling deeper into the darkness.

"Get them both!" Sean roared, and a burst of gunshots strafed the hillside.

Then bright lights hit the men. "Federal agents! Drop your weapons!" Scuffling sounds followed—guns hitting concrete, voices snapping orders, bodies shoved to the ground, handcuffs clicking.

"Saldana, Parker, come on out," Kramer called.

Natalia lifted her head, then eased to her feet. She slipped and slid the rest of the way down the levee, reaching the walkway at the same time Josh emerged from the trees. She took a few halting steps toward him before breaking into a run. He met her halfway, wrapping his arms around her, holding her as tightly as she clung to him.

"You're all right," she whispered, pressing her face against his neck.

"You scared ten years off my freaking life! Why did you follow us? They would have killed you!"

"From where I stood, it looked like they were about to kill *you*." She drew back, then touched his face. "I couldn't let that happen. I—I—" Tears welled and a knot formed in her throat. She hadn't said the words since she was eight years old, and they were tough. God, much tougher than she'd expected.

Josh's features softened, and he brushed her hair back before placing a kiss on her forehead. "I love you, Natalia. I always have. And you don't have to say it back, because I know. I've always known."

She gazed at him a moment, overawed by the simple trust and faith in his words. "I love you, Josh." She whispered it, then said it again louder. Surer. "I love you."

He lifted her off her feet, swung her around in a circle, then kissed her, hungry, greedy, stealing the few bits of words that escaped her lips. *Love...love...I love...*

Heat spread through her, sweet, chasing away chills that had hidden inside her forever. She felt freer, younger, lighter—the way she imagined a normal woman must feel. And hopeful. Oh, so hopeful. It was Christmas Eve. She loved Josh and he loved her back. Anything was possible.

Kramer cleared his throat. "Come on, guys, we've got work to do here."

Reluctantly they broke off the kiss, but Josh didn't let her go. He wrapped his arm around her waist and held her close to his side, and she held on to him, too.

"You might want to get hold of Thomas Smith," Josh said. "He's with the U.S. Attorney's office in Chicago. Tell him Merry Christmas. I'm going to testify."

Natalia looked sharply at him. She had a pretty good idea when and why he'd come to that decision, but her decision trumped his. "Don't bother. I've already offered the U.S. Attorney a deal that I'll testify against the Mulroneys if they leave you alone."

He looked stunned. "You can't do that."

"I can."

"You don't know the stuff I know."

"I know an awful lot that you don't know." She smiled hesitantly. "You were only one of the semi-bad guys, remember? I *was* one of the bad guys."

Kramer rubbed his temple as if his head hurt. "Look, I'd like to get home at least long enough to deliver my kids' Santa gifts before they wake up tomorrow. Besides, it may be a moot point. These guys tried to murder both of you in front of a dozen federal and local authorities. They're probably not going back to Chicago until they've been tried for tonight and for those attempted murders back in the summer. Depending on the sentences they get here, they may never get back to Chicago."

His implication took a moment to sink in. Natalia looked from him to the other men busy around them. "You mean you're not taking us into custody? We're free to go?"

"Yes and no. We're not taking you, but I've got orders to turn you over to someone else. How much freedom you have with her is anyone's guess." He gestured toward the park entrance, where officers let two people pass.

Pregnant or not, Liz Saldana still moved with an inherent grace and sexiness that made Natalia feel like a newborn colt. She dropped her husband's hand and reached them with arms open wide, gathering them both into a sweetly coffee-scented embrace. An instant later, Joe joined the group hug. "You're safe," he said, his voice husky.

Safe. So that's what this sensation is. She'd spent so much of her life hiding and running. Now she didn't have to do that anymore. She had Josh, his family, normalcy and hope.

"…got a suite at a hotel not far," Liz was saying. "We'll spend the night there, and tomorrow morning we'll get an early start for Savannah. Your parents are going to be so thrilled…"

Natalia let the words flow on as she gazed skyward. The snow the forecasters had been predicting was coming down, big, fat flakes that drifted lazily, catching in their hair, on their clothes, their smiles. From somewhere came church bells, accompanied by the sound of carolers. *O holy night…*

She smiled at Josh, and he sweetly, intimately smiled back. He knew what she was feeling, what she was thinking, and she loved him even more for it.

They had their very own Christmas miracle.

* * * * *

SECOND-CHANCE SHERIFF

Linda Conrad

To Christmas lovers everywhere.
And especially to Keyren Gerlach, Marilyn Pappano
and Loreth Anne White!

Have a safe, loving and joyous holiday season!

Chapter 1

Oh, dear God, not now.

Cameron Farrell's knuckles whitened on the steering wheel as his rear tires spun uselessly, slipping and sliding on hidden patches of ice. He hadn't thought it necessary to engage the four-wheel drive when they'd set out from his place on the mountaintop only a few minutes ago. The long driveway could be treacherous this time of year, but it was as familiar to him as the sky over his childhood home.

Still, typical of December weather on the western slope of the Colorado Rockies, the snowstorm they'd been expecting for tomorrow was heading in early. Things had gone from bad to worse in an instant.

Navigating the narrowest spot, with steep cliffs on both sides, Cam was afraid to take his hands off the wheel. Better wait for the public road and a more wide-open spot to reach down and flip the four-wheel drive switch.

"Daddy! Are those snowflakes?"

Cam flicked a glance in the rearview mirror and saw his nearly four-year-old daughter buckled securely in her child safety seat. She was pointing out the window. Her blue eyes were wide and full of joy, and her straw-colored hair was tucked up tightly under her fake bunny-fur cap.

Just gazing at her beautiful face brought a familiar ache to his chest. Every day she grew more and more to look like her mother, the woman who'd died giving birth to her.

He loved his only daughter and would protect her with his life. And guilt was responsible for his pain—not the girl. But knowing that didn't seem to make a difference. It was like being caught up in a tornado of emotion he could do nothing to stop. Cam knew their time was running short. If he didn't take a break from his own child soon, their relationship might be ruined forever.

"Yes, Chloe, those are snowflakes," he said, trying his best to temper the tone of his voice as he hit the public road and flipped the four-wheel switch. "Don't you remember snow from last year?"

"No, Daddy. Will it be a white Christmas like in Nana's pretty song, do you think?"

Damned Patricia Connolly's meddling, anyway. As much as he appreciated her help and concern, his mother-in-law and her sentimentality drove him nuts. He would be perfectly happy forgetting about the holiday all together. He had no pleasant memories of Christmas and would be just fine doing without the songs and the lights, the music and the mush.

"The weather reports say we're in for a good snow. I imagine it will stick around the whole week 'til Christmas day."

"Yippee! Can we build a snowman? Will I be home?"

"We've already talked about this, Chloe Amanda. Your grandmother wants you to spend your birthday and the holiday at her house. She wants to throw a birthday party for you. All your friends from playschool will be there. That's why we packed your overnight bag and brought your doll along. You like it at Nana's. And you love your grandparents. I know you do."

"Yes, Daddy. I like it there. But I want to be home with you.

Who's going to spend Christmas with you if I'm with Nana and Grandpa? Will you come for my birthday party?"

"No, I have to stay at home to take care of the animals." That was as good an excuse to be alone as any. "You remember that Maxine and Jim have the week off. You waved goodbye. Who would take care of the lambs and chickens if I left?"

Cam had taken pains to arrange for his housekeeper and farmhand to take off so he didn't have to face anyone on Christmas Eve. He would much prefer to spend the time by himself, toasting the good woman he'd lost four years ago that night.

He glanced in the mirror again and saw Chloe pouting. What a beautiful child she was. Even when she was throwing a tantrum or crying, she simply glowed with beauty and good spirit. It ripped his heart out not to be able to hold her in his arms. To be the daddy she so desperately needed. But he couldn't bear it. He just couldn't.

Instead, his housekeeper, Maxine, did the hugging. And his mother-in-law gladly stepped up in the hugs and kisses department. The tension between him and Chloe was building fast. He knew he had to act now. His daughter deserved the best life he could provide. And that didn't include living with a shell of a man.

"I had another dream about my mommy." Chloe's voice was soft and tenuous. She knew he didn't like it when she talked about her mother.

Like the talk about Christmas snow, this was one more problem his mother-in-law had brought down upon them. Constantly talking about Mandy and showing Chloe pictures of her dead mother was not helpful. He knew Patricia meant well, but what good did it do?

None. All this talk was only causing Chloe to have bad dreams about a mother that she had never met. He would have to speak to Pat again about keeping Chloe grounded in the present and thinking about the future instead of dwelling on the past. He did plenty enough of that for all of them.

"I really wish you'd…"

"But, Daddy, Mommy said she was sending me a Christmas angel to be my new mama."

Sighing, Cam lowered his voice. "Chloe, would you like to live with Nana and Grandpa permanently and have Nana be your new mama? You love them. Think of all the fun you would have. Plus, next year when you go to school, you'll be able to walk from their house instead of taking a bus. Wouldn't that be fun?"

"I guess so. But I wouldn't mind the bus. And who's going to take care of you?"

Not waiting for the same boring answer he always gave when she asked things like that, Chloe sat back in her seat and pouted. Cam stayed silent, watching the heavy white snow falling against the backdrop of green spruce and pine covering his grandfather's mountaintop.

He loved this mountain and his family's home here. Most of his school years had been spent living down in the valley in the tourist town of Juniper with his parents, or off in the East at college. But his heart had always remained rooted in the deep forests and valley views of the large home and small farm his grandfather had built.

He never wanted to leave for long.

But the Farrell family was nearly all gone now. His grandparents gone due to natural causes and his parents taken by a deadly airplane accident. He missed them all. Chloe was the only real family he had left, and he couldn't stand being around her for very long at any one time. Just as well. He wasn't fit company for anyone, let alone a child, on most days.

When his in-laws had permanently moved to Juniper after Mandy died, Pat had said he should feel like a part of their family. She'd offered him a home. He liked Pat and Robert well enough. They were kind souls who'd lost their only daughter on the day he'd lost his wife.

But nothing had felt right to him when he'd tried to move in with them in Juniper after his rehab. Nowhere else on earth could ever be truly home except up here in the isolation and stark beauty of his family's mountain. The peace and the magnificent charm went a long way toward healing his body, if not his soul.

When he'd been well enough, he'd brought his baby daughter up to the mountain. They'd had plenty of help and his in-laws were always near when he needed them. But recently, taking care of a growing, needy daughter had become too difficult. Especially when it hurt so much just to look at her.

His tires slipped against another hidden patch of ice and Cam was forced to give his full concentration to navigating the long, narrow road down the mountainside. He'd hoped he could make it to Juniper and drop off Chloe before the worst of the storm made climbing back up this road totally impossible. He was determined to spend the holiday alone, as usual.

Tara Jackson hung on to her steering wheel for dear life. That same car was following her again. And now it was snowing and the roads to Cam Farrell's home were slippery as hell.

It had been ten long years since the last time she'd come this way. Once upon a time she had even lived in Cam's grandfather's house on the mountaintop. As Tara gingerly stepped on the gas, hoping her tires wouldn't come out from under her on the ice before she could reach the safety of the Farrell home and Cam's help, she wondered if she would make it before her stalker caught up.

She had to. Not much question in her mind about why she was being followed. Her boss had probably guessed that she was a spy for the governor, and then had put a contract out on her. If she didn't reach Cam's place before the hitman reached her, she would never live to see Cam or anyone else again.

Glancing down at her backpack in the bucket seat beside her, she figured her boss, the Colorado attorney general, would also sincerely love to get his hands on the computer thumb drive she'd hidden in with her extra underwear, makeup and her .38. The computer drive contained proof of his criminal activities. She'd worked hard over the last year, gathering enough evidence, and her undercover investigation was almost over.

Tara had hoped to reach the governor with her information today. After talking to the governor in person and turning over her evidence, she would then be able to take the necessary steps to hide until the attorney general and his cohorts were behind bars.

Unfortunately, it was looking more and more like she would not be talking to the governor today. And judging by the weather, she would be damned lucky to make it to the top of this mountain in one piece.

Cam was her best hope. He was the closest lawman she knew she could trust. Everyone else was suspect.

She hadn't seen Cam in nearly ten years, but knew he had graduated from college and run for county sheriff—winning in a landslide. Tara had always thought being the sheriff was a perfect job for Cam. He was honest and strong, and truly cared for people's welfare—though she also knew his long-term goals were more political. Cam's dream as a boy had been someday running for the United States Senate like his father, Wild Bill Farrell.

A senate seat had been his father's dream for Cam, too. And was the whole reason why she and Cam weren't still together today.

As usual, a ten-year-old ache came back to drive a stake into her heart whenever she thought back to their breakup and his parents' role in it. Tara forced a deep breath of air into her lungs and pushed away the painful memories. She wasn't going to a sweethearts reunion and needed to remember that. No, this was a life or death mission. When she'd turned off the highway and headed for Cam's, she had committed. Now she had no other choice.

Besides, the last thing she'd heard of Cam was when his parents had been killed in a private airplane crash in the mountains. At that time, nearly five years ago, the papers stated that Cam was married and his wife was expecting a child. Tara had tried then to push him out of her mind for good. But she'd been trying unsuccessfully to do just that for the last ten years with little luck.

The only thing saving her sanity was her work. With other things to worry about, she didn't think of her lost lover every minute.

But today she desperately needed help from somewhere. And Cam was the closest lawman she dared trust.

She sure hoped his family still lived on this mountain and that they hadn't gone away for the holidays. With the reminder of the time of year, Tara thought back to the many wonderful Christmases they'd spent with Cam's grandparents up on this mountain. The Farrell family home had always been filled with music and laughter and warmth. So unlike her own desolate and lonely home—at any time of year.

A loud *ping* hitting the trunk of her car snapped Tara out of her reverie. She glanced in the mirror and nearly peed her pants.

That was the sound of a bullet! Now that they'd driven off the main highway and into this isolated country, the hitman was taking his chances. Even through the falling snow she saw his gun arm hanging out the window with the barrel pointed directly at her car.

She stepped down hard on the gas as her entire back window exploded in a shower of breaking glass. Shrieking in terror, she pushed even harder on the gas and jerked against the wheel without thinking.

She only knew that she had to get away.

Her tires began to slip and the car spun sideways, crashing off the roadway and into blowing snow and trees. Everything around her was white for a moment. But the next thing she knew, a forest of trees loomed directly ahead. She tried steering, but it was a lost cause.

Still high on the mountain, but now on the two-lane public road, Cam felt more in control.

"Daddy, look! There's my Christmas angel! Stop!"

"Chloe, please. I can't stop here. There's a car coming around the bend. See the headlights?"

"But she's in trouble, Daddy. We need to help her."

Cam seldom indulged his child in her many fantasies the way her grandmother did, but this time the tone of her voice was urgent. Still, as narrow as the road was and as dangerous the icy patches, it was impossible to stop. He hoped the other driver was going slow enough to avoid a collision.

"You must've fallen asleep and dreamed the angel, Chloe. You know angels aren't real. There's nothing there. Daddy has to pay attention to the road now. Please calm down."

"But, Daddy…"

"Not now, Chloe."

The other car kicked up a cloud of snow as it sped by, going way too fast for the conditions. It just missed slamming into the side of his SUV but the driver never slowed for a moment. Cam didn't get a good look at the driver but he knew none of his neighbors drove a car like that. If this was a visitor to the mountain, he'd picked the wrong day and would probably end up headfirst into a tree before he reached his destination.

With both hands back on the wheel, Cam entered the next curve in the road. He'd already engaged the four-wheel drive, but these damned icy patches were still treacherous.

As his headlights rounded the turn, Cam saw something terrible and his breath caught. Another car had tried to make the curve too fast and was crashed headfirst into a tree.

There was nothing to do now but stop. Cam couldn't leave anyone stranded in a snow drift in this kind of weather. Even if it turned out to be a drunk. Because drunks had families too.

He found a straighter patch of road so his SUV could be spotted before anyone rammed into it blind. Stopping as far off the road as possible, Cam put it in park but left the engine running and the heat blasting.

"Stay here, Chloe. I'm going back to check on the people in that wrecked car. I hope no one was badly injured. It'll be tough getting an ambulance up here in the storm."

"Maybe you'll see my angel, Daddy. Help her too. She needs us."

Cam swore under his breath. This angel business was all he needed today. "Just stay put, young lady."

As he wrenched open his door and stepped out into the wind, Cam's right knee almost gave out on him, reminding him of why he was no longer a sheriff. Mostly healed after years of rehab, his shattered kneecap had nevertheless gone a long way toward ending his career in law enforcement. The recurring stiffness when the weather turned cold and wet was also a painful reminder of why he hated Christmas Eve.

Cam ignored the ache and carefully limped his way off the road and plowed through snow and brush into the trees. The closer he came to the car, the more his instincts were screaming at him that something was very wrong. Things were too still. Too quiet.

He hoped to hell no one had died in the wreck. What would he tell Chloe?

Calling out, he was forced to give up when the wind killed any sound. By the time he was five feet behind the car, he could see something that made the hair on the back of his neck stand up. On the car's trunk, both fenders and the shattered back window—bullet holes.

Hesitating, he checked his surroundings and looked back to the road. Chloe and the SUV seemed safe and sound where he'd left them. Nothing was stirring in the woods. This was the first time since he'd become disabled and gave up his job that Cam wished he still carried a weapon. He wondered what kind of tragedy he would find when he checked the driver's seat.

But things were quiet. Had this happened last night?

Dreading what he must do, Cam plowed around the car to the driver's side. He couldn't see a thing through the new snow clogging up the view to inside.

He tried the door and found it ajar, telling him that the driver had either gotten out of the car or someone had already found the wreck and opened the door from the outside. Either way, he wasn't surprised when he pulled on the door handle—and found the seat empty.

He also wasn't terribly surprised to find a small amount of

blood. On the steering wheel and inside on the door handle. Was it from the accident? Or from the bullets?

The blood looked fresh. He tore off his glove, reached around and laid his hand flat on the hood. Still warm. Considering the growing windchill, this car hadn't been sitting here for too long.

But where was the driver now?

Turning in a wide circle, Cam thought back to the speeding car he'd met on the road. He was absolutely positive there had only been one person in that car—the driver. And if an injured person was lying down in the backseat, and the driver had been speeding and hoping to make it to a hospital, they were crazy for going *up* the mountain road instead of back down to town.

That whole idea seemed too outrageous to contemplate seriously—even for lost tourists. But then why…?

Cam looked toward the woods, wishing he could take the time to do a thorough search for survivors. But the storm was getting worse by the minute and he needed to get Chloe off the mountain.

After tramping his way back to the SUV, he slipped into the driver's seat without letting in more than a handful of blowing snow. "You okay back there, Chloe?"

"Did you see my angel, Daddy? Was she all right?"

"No angels. In fact, I didn't see anyone."

Chloe began to whimper and Cam gritted his teeth. "If what you thought you saw was really an angel, she can take care of herself. Maybe she flew up to heaven."

"Do you think so?"

"I'm sure of it. Now you be a good girl and stay quiet while I call Sheriff Reiner to report the…uh…incident." In the rearview mirror, he saw Chloe nod and then stare out the window and up at the sky.

Cam flipped open his cell, only to find it had no bars. The storm must be interfering with reception. Irritated, he stuck the phone on the seat beside him and put the SUV into gear.

It would take an hour to go the usual twenty-minute distance down to Juniper in this weather. But he had no choice. He planned to stop every fifteen minutes and check the phone.

Cam tried to concentrate on his driving. But he couldn't stand the idea of someone possibly lying in the woods bleeding to death while he could do nothing about it.

Chapter 2

Standing in his mother-in-law's foyer with Stetson in hand, Cam shifted from one foot to the other, fighting to excuse himself and leave as soon as possible. "Jingle Bells" was playing through the sound system. Mistletoe over the door, decorated pine wreaths and the smell of gingerbread left little doubt about which season was being celebrated in this house.

Christmas was a bigger pain in the ass than ever. The whole thing gave him heartburn.

He wanted to be on his way back up the mountain before the storm got any worse. Along the route, he planned to check on what the sheriff had turned up at the car wreck scene.

"Daddy, come see!" Chloe had dashed into the great room the minute he'd pulled off her coat and handed it over to her grandmother. Now she was calling him to join her.

"I have to be going, Chloe." Cam didn't move but looked helplessly over to Pat, Chloe's grandmother.

"I happen to agree with your daughter, son. You just got here. You haven't even taken off your coat yet. At least have a glass of eggnog."

Cam stared down at his boots, which were dripping on the gleaming cherrywood floor. "I can't stay. I have to make sure the animals are okay and meet the sheriff on the mountain road before this storm socks us in."

Pat tsked at him. "The sheriff can handle that wreck without your help. And your man Jim Tisdale would never walk away from those lambs and chickens and leave you unprepared to last a week. The animals will be fine for a few hours. You just want to be up there alone on your mountaintop to brood over Christmas."

She put her hand on his arm, and lowered her voice. "Amanda's death was not your fault, Cam. She would've died giving birth to Chloe whether you were there with her or not. I miss her, too. Every day. But it's been four years. You can't go on living under a rock and blaming yourself for something you couldn't control. Your daughter needs you, and you need her."

He did not want to talk about this. Not now.

"Let's revisit this discussion in the new year, Pat. I've been thinking about making different arrangements for Chloe and I'd like to run them by you then. But right now I really do have to go before the snow piles up too badly on the narrowest part of drive. Jim isn't there to plow."

"Have you considered staying with…" Pat's words were interrupted by a three-foot-tall tornado.

"Come on, Daddy." Chloe flew into the room, her blond curls swirling around her head, and grabbed his hand. "You really *need* to see this."

She tugged frantically on his hand, and he had little choice but to stumble after her into the great room. "What is so important? I told you I can't stay."

"Look!" She pointed at the Christmas tree, with all its festive twinkling lights and colorful decorations. "That's her."

"What are you talking about? That's Nana's tree. You knew she was decorating a…"

"No, Daddy. Look at the angel. On the very top. That's my angel. The one I saw in the woods. It looks just like her."

At the very tip of the seven-foot-tall tree sat an unusual angel decoration. The feminine form had red hair instead of the typical blond, and small white fairy wings instead of the usual overpowering gauzy attachments. Cam turned back to Pat, who'd followed them into the room.

"New tree decorations?" he asked. "I don't remember that angel. Didn't you always place a star at the top of your tree?"

Pat nodded and looked down at Chloe, who was busy gazing at the angel. "I found a box of old family decorations in the attic a few days ago. Things I hadn't thought of in years. That angel belonged to Amanda. She always loved it as a girl. And I thought…"

"See, Daddy. Mommy sent me an angel. Nana says so, too."

Pat turned to Cam as questions jumped in her eyes. "What is she talking about?"

Cam ignored Pat for the moment and knelt on one knee to speak to his daughter. "We'll talk about this more after Christmas, young lady. But right now I have to go back up the mountain."

"But Daddy…"

"No, Chloe. Not now. I want you to be a good girl for Nana. Don't get your hopes up about finding an angel. Angels aren't for real and you know it."

"But Daddy…" She reached her arms out to him.

Cam stood and backed up a step. "Run upstairs and see if you can find your granddad while I say goodbye to your grandmother."

"Yes, Daddy. I love you." She stuck out her lip.

"Enjoy your birthday and Christmas, Chloe."

"Okay. Bye, Daddy." She hung her head, looking just like he had earlier, and marched toward the stairs.

"I'll be up in minute, Chloe." Pat turned to him with tears in her eyes when the girl was out of earshot. "What was that all about?"

"The angel? Chloe swears her mother came to her in a dream to tell her she was sending an angel to be her new mommy. Now

Chloe is even seeing living angels. Said she saw *her* angel in the woods on the way down here today."

"The child is lonely, Cam. Of course she's dreaming of guardian angels and a new mommy. I'm surprised she hasn't already come up with an imaginary friend or two.

"And what was that look you gave her when all she wanted was a hug from her daddy?" Pat added.

Cam spun around and headed for the door. "I don't have time for this right now. *You* tell her that angels don't exist. Maybe she'll believe you."

As he strode toward the foyer, he kept talking over his shoulder. "Tell Bob I said thanks for keeping her over the holiday and for making her birthday special. The three of you enjoy the party and have a terrific Christmas. I'll call Chloe on her birthday and then see you in a week."

He couldn't get out the door fast enough.

Tara slipped and fell in the snow for the fourth time. She was soaked and freezing after two hours of stumbling through the thick mountain woods in the snow. Her jacket was torn and she had brambles in her hair. But at least she'd apparently given the hitman the slip.

She figured he might still be out there somewhere looking for her, but for now she had a bigger problem. She hadn't thought she could get too lost by going uphill. Cam's family owned the entire top of this mountain. She just had to keep climbing and eventually she'd run into their house and hobby farm. Right?

But nothing was working out for her today. First of all, she'd discovered her cell phone service wasn't available. She couldn't call for help. And then about a half hour ago she had run smack into a barbed-wire fence. The only thing left for her to do was follow the fence line until she ran into a road or driveway.

Not crazy about moving out in the open instead of sneaking through the woods, Tara hoped this fence belonged to Cam. She'd finally remembered the entryway to his property as being a long, narrow road that wound down through a deep canyon with steep cliffs on either side. All in all, as tired as she was at this point, traveling up his cleared drive instead of trying to climb those cliffs seemed like a much better idea.

If…she could just avoid the hitman while she was doing it. And if she could stay on her feet in these rocky woods while she followed the fence. Which was looking more and more doubtful as the snow piled up and taking each breath felt as though her lungs were being ripped apart from the inside out.

Her feet were half-numb and half burning with the cold. And the backpack straps were digging painfully into her shoulders under the jacket. But she was grateful she'd remembered to snatch it from the front seat as she fled the hitman. She'd taken off through the woods as fast as her scared feet would take her. After everything, it would be terrible to lose that thumb drive.

Oh, God, her fingers and toes were so cold.

Think of something else.

When she tried to blank her mind, the same images entered her thoughts that always came when she least wanted them. *Cam.* And a warm spring day the year she turned sixteen.

She'd been crying. The police had come to cart her father off to jail—yet again. And her mother was preparing to leave Juniper for a new job as a maid in a summer resort in another part of the state. Tara had felt her world crumbling around her.

To get her to stop crying, her best friend, Cam, had quickly promised that she could live with his grandfather in the house on the mountain. It was a big enough place, he'd said, and his grandfather, a recent widower, wouldn't mind. She could still go to high school in Juniper and be close to her few friends. She was so relieved that she'd kissed him for the first time.

That was it for her. She knew for sure then that she loved Cam Farrell and had felt it would last forever.

Cam looked terribly handsome that day, with the sunshine shooting rich, red highlights into his sandy-brown hair, and those green eyes of his flashing looks at her that made her squirm with emotions she couldn't name at age sixteen.

"I love you with every fiber of my being," he'd said

dramatically as he held her in his arms. "You are my whole world. I'll never leave you, Tara. I swear it on my grandfather's life. As long as I'm alive, you will never feel alone again."

The more Tara saw Cam, the more she was sure that she wanted to be with him forever, even though it seemed impossible with their backgrounds. She loved everything about him. He was warm and giving and thoughtful. And he'd treated her with respect. At first she'd secretly wondered if what she felt was simply gratitude. But as the next year of school flew by and they became closer—and more intimate—she found out exactly how real her love for Cam could be.

Thoughts of him filled her mind morning, noon and night. He even occupied her dreams. She spent all her downtime building future castles in the air with him as the center of her life.

They would have children with spectacular green eyes. And a cozy, permanent home to call their own. Even grandchildren some day.

Maybe that was the biggest reason why, when it all came crashing down around her, she had felt so devastated. He hadn't believed she was telling the truth. She remembered the fury and the hurt like it had only happened moments ago. He'd chosen his parents' version of things over hers—despite her pleading with him to believe and trust in her. She had not taken money from the Farrells for school.

In her most secret moments, she had always harbored the hope that time would bring him back to her eventually. That he would show up some day and apologize. She couldn't quite accept that he'd meant what he said.

"I believe you're lying." He'd said those words with huge unshed tears in his tender eyes. "You're ripping my heart out. I never want to see you again."

She hadn't stopped crying for two years afterward. But the flame of hope had burned on anyway. Until she'd read about his parents' death, and saw the news article mentioning his pregnant wife.

It had been a reality check. A reminder of who she was.

But she would never stop loving him. She knew that for sure, because she had tried many times since then. She'd even become engaged once in the hopes that someone else's love could wash away the love she still felt for Cam. It hadn't worked. Her love for Cam was apparently so deep in her that she'd hurt another good man whose only fault had been trying to make her happy.

Sighing and shaking her head, Tara looked up suddenly and realized she couldn't see the fence anymore. She couldn't see much of anything past ten feet in any direction. The snow was coming down by the bucketful. Was she at the driveway?

She took a couple of steps that felt as though she were going up the mountain and turned in a circle. She'd expected to hit something hard under her feet when she reached the driveway. She had even wondered if there might have been a new gate put in some time over the ten years since she'd last been here. But now she couldn't see or feel anything.

Good Lord. Could she be lost in a whiteout? Would she freeze to death out here on Cam's mountain before the blizzard stopped?

As tough as Tara had made herself over the last few years, she still felt the tears threatening to make matters even worse. *Oh, Cam, I really need you.*

All of a sudden, out of the snowy darkness, a light hit her face. As she squinted to see what was happening, another light appeared through the snowflakes and she realized they were a car's headlights.

Oh, no. The hitman had found her after all.

Hide. Without looking, she jumped as far as she could to the side and away from the lights—and landed all wrong. Her ankle screamed in pain and she found herself lying flat in a ditch filled with cold, wet snow. But she knew there could be no stopping or she would end up dead. Crawling on her hands and knees, she tried to scramble away. But her hand landed on thin air, and she felt herself falling, tumbling.

Down and down she went. And then there was nothing in her world at all but the cold and darkness.

* * *

Cam couldn't believe his eyes. There was a woman walking on his driveway in this blizzard. At least he thought it was a woman. When he'd first spotted her and put on his brakes, he could've sworn he was seeing Chloe's angel.

But the more he considered it, the more he decided what he'd been seeing was a very real redheaded woman in a silver-hooded parka with a tan backpack strapped to her shoulders. Staring out the window, he found he couldn't even see her anymore. She'd disappeared into the snow-filled ditch beside the road, and now blowing snow was covering her trail. But here, just inside his gate, he knew that ditch led to a dangerous four-foot drop.

Had she hurt herself? What the heck was a woman doing out in this kind of weather? Damn.

Ramming his SUV into park but leaving it on with the heater blasting, Cam leaned heavily against the door and opened it to the gale-force winds. This might be the stupidest move he'd made in a long time, but he couldn't simply drive away without finding out if the woman was hurt.

She was probably crazy as a loon. But that was no reason to leave her out here to die in the elements. *Hell.* He'd left the sheriff still searching back down the road so he could make it to the top of the mountain while it was feasible.

There went his quiet evening in isolation.

He pulled his Stetson lower and flipped up the collar on his cowhide coat, fighting his way over to the side of the road. But he couldn't see to the bottom of the ditch through the damned heavy snowfall.

Double hell.

He had no choice but to climb down into the deepest part of the ditch and see if he could spot her. Cam carefully eased along the part of the ditch that sloped the least, hoping his bum knee would hold him up as he tested each step for stability. The wind was blowing hard enough to cover this section of ditch with more than a foot of drifting snow within five minutes, so he pushed himself harder.

Needing to find her and get back on the road before his driveway became impassable, Cam had almost given up when he spotted something shiny under a thin blanket of new snow.

The woman was lying facedown, apparently unconscious. Was she drunk? Just what he needed.

Triple hell.

He bent and pulled her into his arms, then turned and immediately started back up the bank toward his waiting SUV. Featherlight, even with the oversize backpack, she wasn't difficult to carry. But still Cam was careful to watch every step with his bad knee.

Hitting level ground in front of the SUV, he started around to the passenger door as fast as he dared on the slick surface. When the woman groaned and stirred in his arms, he was afraid she might bolt and take them both down.

"Easy does it," he murmured. "You'll be safe."

"Cam?"

The sound of his name on her lips drew his attention to her face. With one glance, shock jolted down his spine and he faltered midstep. He stared into the face he had sworn never to see again—but nevertheless saw nearly every night in his dreams.

The moment he gazed at the familiar face, his heart slammed against his rib cage and the blood drained from his head. The skin on her cheeks was turning a sickly blue. She tried to open her eyes but couldn't seem to focus.

Light-headed, he stumbled against the door. "Tara?"

"Cam, help me," she cried weakly.

Regardless of how he felt about her, he had no choice.

"Almost there." He recovered his equilibrium and managed to force open the passenger door.

As he placed her limp body into the seat and buckled her in, he noticed a gash on her head and a lot of blood splatter on her parka. It was possible her injuries had been caused by her tumble into the ditch. But it was also possible she had been one of the people from the abandoned car that he knew the sheriff was still searching for in the woods.

Cam didn't like the idea of either one. There would be no possibility of taking her to the hospital tonight. No vehicles could make it up or down this mountain, at least until the snow stopped falling and the plows came out. And what if someone had been shooting at her? Where was that someone now?

As he made his way around the front of the SUV again, he found himself wishing this was only a bad dream. His life had suddenly gone from depressing and annoying to disturbed and conflicted all in the space of two or three ill-considered moves. He should've kept driving. He'd be almost home by now. But no matter what else he was or had become, he knew such a thing was not in him.

Climbing into the driver's seat and carefully releasing the brake, Cam tried to control his swirling thoughts. As a youth he had been so dead sure that life was his for the taking. Nothing bad could ever touch the beloved only son of the great William "Wild Bill" Farrell.

He'd had it all. A beautiful and loving girlfriend. The best grades in his class. A rich United States senator for a father. He was the golden boy who never stepped into dark places. His life had spread out before him like a juicy watermelon ripe for the eating.

As high as he was then, Cam never considered how far he might fall.

The SUV's tires suddenly slid against another patch of ice and all Cam could think of was that he couldn't lose control and put the SUV into a drift. As hard as it was snowing, it wouldn't be long before nothing but a snowplow would make it through to the house.

Hanging on to the steering wheel with both hands, he took a quick glance over at Tara, still slumped in the seat. Now that he'd made the mistake of picking her up, he was determined to see her live through this.

That is, before he packed her up and sent out of his life again—for good.

Chapter 3

"Take it easy, Tara. You're safe."

Cam kicked the front door closed behind him with his bad leg and pushed through to the great room, still carrying Tara in his arms. She was incoherent and he worried she was going into shock. After removing her backpack and laying her out on the long leather couch in front of the fireplace, he pulled a wool throw off a chair and gently covered her. Kneeling before the hearth, he prepared to light the kindling.

He'd already decided that Tara wasn't seriously injured. One of the gashes on her cheek might need a stitch or two, but the others were all superficial and would respond to a careful cleansing and some antiseptic.

But, dammit, just how long would it be before he could be rid of her again?

He still needed to check her toes and fingers for frostbite. Cam hoped to hell that wouldn't be a problem. He knew how to treat frostbite. You couldn't live all your life in the Colorado Rockies without learning. But he also knew the pain involved was severe.

"Where are we? Your house? Are all the doors locked?" Tara was still on the couch, but she was attempting to focus her eyes and fighting to sit up.

"Stay still. Don't move yet." He checked on her over his shoulder as he made sure the kindling had ignited.

Tara groaned, but she also quit struggling to sit up and fell back against the leather. "Check the doors, Cam."

"All the doors and windows are secure. The house is wired for security. Relax while you warm up."

Her eyes were open again. "I'll be fine."

Cam carefully began pulling off her boots. Frostbite was the biggest potential danger. Her socks were dry, but she winced as he gently removed them. Another good sign.

"Your feet and hands are going to hurt while they warm up," he told her. "But they look good. You might have a little frostnip, but I doubt anything will blister. We need to get hot liquid down you and your cuts should be treated.

"I swear you're safe," he added, more to keep her quiet than anything else.

"But I have to tell you…"

"Hold those thoughts." He slipped a pillow under her feet and hurried into the kitchen to put on the kettle and retrieve the first aid kit.

By the time he returned with the kit and a steaming mug of hot herbal tea, Tara was sitting up. Her feet were still elevated on the couch and she was in the process of pulling off her gloves.

"Was I ever glad to see you," she said when she looked up. "I thought I was dead for sure. Where's my backpack?"

He nodded to the pack, sitting on the floor beside the hearth and handed her the mug. "Here. Drink this down before you do anything else."

She flicked a glance at the pack then tried to grab the mug's handle, but her fingers wouldn't do as she asked.

"Hold on with both palms and let the heat of the mug warm your hands. You didn't notice any frostbite on your fingertips, did you?"

Shaking her head, she said, "They're white and numb, but nothing is blue. Judging from how badly they throb, I would bet none of them are frosted. I wouldn't vouch the same for the tip of my nose, however."

"We'll keep an eye on it. You were lucky. The temperature is moving even lower now as the winds pick up."

She was also lucky that he'd come across her when he had. Or in short order hyperthermia would've set in.

"What happened to your car?" He didn't wait for an answer. "And what are you doing on Farrell Mountain in a snowstorm? I haven't heard a thing from you in ten years."

"I came here to see you."

His heart jumped at her words, but he gritted his teeth and tried to find a little righteous anger. "Ever heard of calling ahead?"

If she'd called and asked to see him, Cam would have warned her off. Apart from the currently dangerous snowstorm swirling around his mountain, he could've told her not to bother. He had nothing to say to her after all this time.

"It's a long story, Cam. I didn't come for a reunion. I came here seeking help from the sheriff."

Hunkering down on his heels beside the couch, he opened the first aid kit. "I haven't been the sheriff for the last four years, Tara. You endangered your life in a snowstorm for no reason."

She looked surprised but recovered quickly. "You were still my best bet for protection. I don't trust anyone else. Besides, you were close by. I was trying to shake the man following me. He wants to kill me."

"Was that your car on the public road with the bullet holes?"

She nodded and closed her eyes. "I thought I was dead for sure this time."

Filing the "this time" remark for later, Cam pulled supplies out of the first aid kit and put a little antiseptic on a swab of cotton. "I need to tend your cuts. Hold still." She wasn't making much sense. What on earth had she gotten herself into?

"Can you do it while I talk?"

He grabbed her chin and held her still. "Shut up for one more minute and let me finish tending your face. Then tell your story."

Curious, but more annoyed at the intrusion from his past, Cam carefully cleaned her cuts. Only one was deep enough to need a butterfly bandage. The rest were minor and would heal with no trouble. Too bad his heart hadn't healed from her betrayal the same way.

He distinctly remembered those first long years of misery, the endless days and sleepless nights after he'd sent her away. Just thinking of it now put a pain in his chest that wouldn't stop.

"Facial cuts are done," he told her as he sat back and checked his work. "And your nose is turning red. It'll be okay, too. Any other cuts?"

"Everything else was covered." She shrugged out of her jacket. "But this parka is definitely ruined. Too bad. It was a lifesaver."

"Tell me about the man who shot at you."

"A hired killer. Don't know his name. But I'm fairly sure there's a contract out on my life. If it wasn't him, it would be another."

"Why?" This wasn't becoming any clearer. "What the hell have you been doing?"

"I've been undercover."

If she'd said she was Chloe's angel, Tara couldn't have surprised him more. "Maybe you'd better start at the beginning." He dragged a chair closer.

"I will. But I think we'd better call for reinforcements first. That guy is probably still out there. Is the new sheriff someone you can trust?"

"Definitely. I've known him for years."

"My cell isn't working due to the storm, I'd guess. Have a landline?"

Cam nodded and went to the desk in the corner. "I saw Sheriff Reiner on the way in just now. He'd been searching the area near your totaled car to find any survivors. But his department's having a real bad day. People are always getting stuck or lost in storms like this one. Hearing about a hired killer in his territory won't help matters."

Picking up the desk phone, Cam was surprised to find it dead. "I guess the landlines are all down with the storm, too. I'm afraid we're on our own."

"Maybe you and I can take care of ourselves, Cam. But I'm worried about your family. What are they…?'"

He stopped her with a raised hand. "We're in the house alone. It's just us."

Tara suddenly looked stricken. As though that was a situation she had never considered.

As he opened his mouth to explain, the lights flickered and then the room went dark save for the light from the fireplace.

Tara couldn't help the gasp that escaped her lips. "Is that normal? Or should I be worried about the killer coming for me in the dark?"

"It's probably storm-related." He turned and headed to the foyer. "I'll get my coat and turn on the generator. Afterward, I'll give the outside a once-over. If anyone is out there, they'll be suffering from the weather. While I was making your tea, the TV news predicted another twenty inches tonight. No one will be able to get in or out of this property until the storm stops."

Horrified at the prospect of being stranded here with a killer stalking her outside and a sexy but annoyed ex-lover inside, Tara watched Cam while he donned his coat, hat and a pair of snow boots.

"Stay by the fire and make yourself at home," he told her as he headed for the kitchen. "I need to check on the animals' welfare after I get the generator up and running. But I won't be long.

"When I get back," he continued, "I want to hear all the details on this undercover operation of yours." Shaking his head as though the idea of her undercover was absolutely absurd, Cam disappeared around the corner.

Tara didn't know whether to be insulted or scared. She'd been so sure that Cam's whole family would be here for the holidays. It had never occurred to her that the two of them would be isolated together—alone.

Facing a hitman might be preferable.

Needing to move around so she could think her predicament through, Tara tested her feet by placing one down on the hardwood floor. Man, that hurt like the devil. She was sure glad she'd thought to put on her padded socks under her boots and jeans before she'd left her apartment this morning and headed out for the governor's vacation home in Aspen. If the governor had still been in Denver instead of spending the holidays with his family, she might've been dressed in something totally unsuitable.

Brrr. The idea gave her chills. She could be worrying about losing her feet to frostbite instead of fussing about spending time alone with an old boyfriend.

An old *married* boyfriend.

The stabbing pain in the bottom of her foot became bearable, so she put the other one down on the floor next to it. Yipes. She had to bite her lip to keep from screaming. But within minutes she felt stronger and more stable. Maybe she was going to live through the experience after all.

As she straightened and looked around the great room, the lights came back on. Then she heard the heater cycling on in another part of the house. She wondered how long the generator would last without running out of fuel.

She went to the fireplace, added a few more logs and stirred the fire. Soon it was blazing.

Looking around the room again, Tara finally realized what she was seeing. Or not seeing. She'd been to Cam's home during the holidays many times growing up. Back then, the whole place had glowed with decorations, lovingly put up by Cam's grandparents. Festive lights, wrapped packages and yummy smells coming from the kitchen. Those were some of the clearest memories from her childhood.

Yet today, a few days before Christmas, this great room was empty of everything but furniture. Except for the roaring fire, it might as well be August.

Where was the tree? Where were the wreaths and holly?

Wandering from room to room downstairs, she searched for anything that said Christmas. With no luck.

Tara easily climbed the stairs to the second floor bedrooms. Surely up here she would find some sign of holiday spirit.

She checked each room as she went down the hall. The first two were guest rooms, and bland. When she came to the room she'd used as a teenager, her hand hesitated on the door handle. Tara wasn't sure she wanted to see this room again after all these years. Too many memories. Both good and bad.

But as the door creaked open, Tara was shocked to see a fantasyland in various shades of pink instead of the cool blues and greens of her youth. The bed was covered with stuffed animals. Yes, this room was most definitely being used by a little girl.

Cam must have a daughter. As Tara moved around the room, she lightly touched the toys and the music boxes. This could be her own little girl's room. If only things had worked out differently.

On top of the dresser, she found several framed photos. A little girl with blond pigtails, holding Cam's hand. An older couple with the same girl at a birthday party. Tara looked around again, but couldn't find any pictures of Cam's wife.

In fact, Tara couldn't remember seeing any pictures of a young woman anywhere in the house. She quickly walked out of the girl's room and headed for the master bedroom. This was going to hurt, but now that she'd thought of it, she needed to see some evidence of the woman who shared her life with Cam.

Tara hesitated once again at the door, but then took a breath and pushed it open. The room that had once belonged to Cam's grandparents had not changed much.

Still the same beige walls. The same heavy, hewn wood furniture. Even the same king-size bed with the thick down-filled mattress.

But there were no photos. None at all that she could see. Not even of the pretty little girl.

Something was wrong in this house. Turning, she headed for the walk-in closet and threw open the doors.

Except for Cam's clothes, the huge closet stood empty. Empty? Was Cam divorced?

"Find what you were looking for?" Cam's voice spun her around.

Busted.

"Cam, where is your wife?"

Furious at the nosy question, Cam said, "Not that it's any of your business, but Mandy died giving birth to my daughter. Four years ago on Christmas Eve."

Tara had the decency to look embarrassed. "Oh, I'm so sorry. This time of year must be terribly hard on you. I…"

"Let's take this discussion down in front of the fire. The generator is set to cycle on and off every two hours to save both propane and the pipes. The great room will remain the warmest part of the house."

He took her by the elbow and ushered her out of his bedroom. Standing in the master bedroom closet, staring at the empty space where Mandy's clothes once hung, was the last place Cam had expected to find Tara. When he was younger, he had dreamed many times of Tara's clothes hanging in a closet next to his. He had built a lot of pipe dreams on that very idea.

Now he refused to succumb to the temptation that her presence ignited. It was wrong of him to still want her as much as he did. Made him feel disloyal to Mandy—a not unfamiliar emotion.

Cam let go of Tara's arm and preceded her down the stairs. Since they were stuck here, she might as well say what she'd come to say. He would listen and then feed her and find her a semi-warm place to sleep until he could get her off his mountain. But that was it.

No reminiscing. No erotic daydreams while she was this close. And absolutely no touching allowed.

"To ease your mind about your pursuer," he began as they hit the bottom of the stairs, "while I was outside, I discovered the driveway has been completely blocked by a small avalanche of snow. Unless the guy can fly through the middle of a deadly storm and land in a thirty-mile-an-hour gale, he will not be getting through."

She put her hand to her heart. "Thank God. Maybe we'll be able to reach the sheriff before the snow stops."

"I want to hear more about it. How are you feeling now? Make yourself comfortable on the couch in front of the fire while I fix us something to eat before the generator shuts down again." He turned away and headed into the open part of the kitchen.

"Uh…how long do you think we'll be stuck?"

Cam pulled a carton of eggs from the fridge, not certain how he should answer. Tara saved him the trouble.

"I know, it depends on the storm. I'm really sorry to be such a bother, Cam. This isn't working out at all the way I pictured when I decided to come to you for help."

"That reminds me. Tell me again why you came here?"

"I think I'd better start at the beginning."

"Go ahead. I can listen and cook at the same time."

He filled the coffeemaker and set it to brew. Then he pulled a pan off the hanging rack, cracked several eggs into a bowl and began to chop a few veggies. His movements were deliberate, economical. Cooking was one of those things he did under duress. But he had been learning to get by with it for the last four years.

Tara stood up and wandered toward the huge open countertop that lay between the kitchen and the great room. "I guess I should start by telling you that I graduated college with a law enforcement degree."

Law enforcement? Another huge surprise from a woman

he'd once thought he knew better than he knew himself. But Cam kept his mouth shut and let her go on with her tale.

She leaned against the counter and watched him work. "I went to work for the state, the CDPS. But shortly afterward I was recruited by the CBI, the Colorado Bureau of Investigation. After a while, I was promoted to a special unit, working under the governor's direction."

"Sounds like you were good at your job." He wasn't surprised. He'd always known Tara was smarter than anyone else imagined.

She shrugged off the compliment. "I guess so. One day the governor called me into his office and told me he had a problem. He'd been approached by someone who supposedly had secret intel on the attorney general. Intel about the AG skimming, not only from his own political action committee, but also from state coffers."

"Isn't the attorney general in charge of the CBI? That would make him your commander."

Tara nodded. "Right. And we'd always gotten along well. This wasn't something I was thrilled to hear, Cam. Believe me. But the governor asked me to go undercover. He wanted me to ask the AG for a job in his election office so I could spy on him and find the facts.

"It meant I had to quit my CBI job and stop outwardly being in law enforcement." She sighed deeply. "I just couldn't turn down the governor, could I?"

"I suppose not. But…"

"Yeah. I had a lot of 'buts' in my mind too. Still, I did it—secretly hoping to find that the intel was wrong. That the AG wasn't a crook. Unfortunately, that hope didn't pan out."

"The AG is skimming?"

"And taking bribes and…well, I have all the pertinent info on a thumb drive and I was on my way to turn it over to the governor. To put an end to the career of a man I had always respected."

Cam's law enforcement training kicked in. "I assume the

AG found out you were spying." He put a mug of coffee down in front of her.

"Yes. I don't know how long he's suspected, but last night I realized someone had been tailing me. I called the governor and he told me to bring the drive to him at his family's vacation home in Aspen without letting on. We still don't know who we can trust.

"Obviously I didn't get there," she said calmly as she took a quick sip of coffee. "I wasn't far from the turnoff for Juniper when I realized I hadn't lost the stalker. I figured my chances of reaching here and maybe shaking the guy first were a heck of a lot better than trying to make it all the way to Aspen."

"And you nearly died trying." He could scarcely believe this was the same girl he used to know.

He plated the eggs and took them to the kitchen table. "Grab the silverware and come eat."

He'd said the words as though the last ten years had never happened. But when she went to the correct drawer with no prompting, the pain reappeared in his chest and a lump as big as the Rockies jumped into his throat.

As Tara sat at the table in her old place, she said. "While we eat, can you tell me about your daughter? About the night your wife died?"

His back went up immediately as he claimed his own chair. "Why? It couldn't matter to you."

"Yeah, it does. Something is still bothering you there. I can tell by the look in your eyes when you mentioned she'd died and by the fact there's no pictures of your wife in the house. I still care about you, Cam."

Talking about his wife's death was the last thing Cam wanted to do. He'd managed to put off the psychiatrists when they'd tried to probe. Rehashing the whole deal now, especially with Tara, was out of the question.

He would tell her no. But knowing Tara, she would keep asking until she finally exposed his sore spots. Hell.

Chapter 4

A few hours after the meal was over and dishes put away, Tara felt groggy from sitting quietly in front of the fireplace. She noticed the couch cushions jiggling under her bottom and when she opened her eyes, Cam was sitting close. He carried two after-dinner glasses, both containing a dark liquid that glowed amber in the firelight.

"You're awake," he said softly. "The electricity is off again and I added logs to the fire. Would you like a glass of brandy?"

"It'll probably knock me out cold, but thanks." She took a tentative sip. "Is everything all right?"

He shrugged and swirled the aged liquid in his glass. "The snow is falling harder now but everything is quiet. I'll probably have to shovel off the porch roof if we get much more of this. Don't want it collapsing."

"Sounds dangerous."

Cam shook his head. "Not really. Are you still tired?"

"Not really." She used his own words and gave him a wry smile. "I've been resting my eyes. Why?"

"Nothing." Cam stared at the brandy in his glass. "So why don't you tell me about your private life. What have you been doing for the last ten years?"

"Are you asking if I'm married or involved?" The idea that he would be curious was intriguing. "I'm neither. Never married. I was too busy working my way through school and then starting my career. Recently, undercover work hasn't left much of an opening for, uh…entanglements."

"I imagine. But about your schooling. I thought—"

Tara felt the heat flare in her face and the anger pushing at her patience, but she fought to bank them. "You thought your parents paid my way through school in return for breaking it off with you. Still believe that? As I tried to tell you then, scholarships and government loans helped me pay my own way. I never took a dime from them."

She caught the surprise and rebuke in Cam's eyes and was about to put up her hackles and continue the fight that had been interrupted ten years ago. But in his typical politically correct style, Cam's face dimpled into a huge grin before she could say a word.

"Good for you for making it through on your own," he murmured. "I always said you were the smart one and a hard worker."

His parents hadn't thought so. They'd been stunned when she turned down their offer of a bribe. That was the only word for what they'd offered. It had made her so angry. And had embarrassed her even though in the end, they were probably right to try ending the relationship.

But his parents were dead now, and she wasn't here to fight with Cam. If he really believed her or not, she needed his help. Moreover, he seemed to need her too. He'd saved her life this afternoon, and Tara wondered if she could do anything to help him in return.

What was he really after with his questions? As a trained investigator, she clearly saw the underlying angst and hunger in his eyes. The hunger she understood. It was everything she could do while sitting beside him not to jump into his arms and rip off his clothes.

As kids they'd been such a hot couple, unable to keep their hands off each other. For years she'd tried to block those images and the fire they'd caused deep inside her gut, but she had never really been successful.

It was the angst in his eyes now that caused her the most concern. Something very strange was going on behind those startling, glacier-green eyes.

She set her glass down on the side table and folded her arms over her breasts in order to keep her hands to herself. "Where's your daughter tonight? Is she safe from the storm?"

His light-green eyes turned deepest emerald, almost black. "Chloe is fine. She's spending her birthday and Christmas with her maternal grandparents down in Juniper."

Look at his eyes. Clearly that was another sore spot. What on earth was going on inside this man whom she had loved nearly all her life?

"Chloe. That's a nice name." Maybe she could get him talking. "Were you planning on joining her in Juniper for the holiday before the snow arrived?" The storm could've put a chink in his plans, too, and that was what was wrong.

"I was on my way back from dropping her off when I spotted you."

"Wait." Tara looked around the room at the obvious lack of Christmas cheer. "You were planning on spending the holidays alone? Up here on the mountaintop with no family and no decorations?"

Sipping his brandy slowly, Cam was quiet a long time. Too long. She was about to ask him something else or to make another remark when he murmured, "It's the way I spend the holidays now. The way I want it. Being alone. I devote Christmas Eve to the memory of my wife. Not with celebrations, but with reflection and contemplation."

Huh? Tara had been a detective too long to take those comments for anything but what they were—guilt. Plain and simple.

Surely she could make Cam explain why, but she'd better take things slow. "How does Chloe feel about you skipping her birthday and Christmas?"

"She doesn't understand. She's too young. But she will some day."

"I see. Do you buy her gifts? Spend time later with her?"

He didn't answer but stood to stir the coals and add another log.

"Four is too young," Tara said, letting him hear the condemnation in her voice. "Too young to understand why her daddy doesn't love her. Why he blames her for her mother's death."

He spun and came back to the couch. "I do love her. But..." When his eyes came up to meet hers through the firelight, his face was full of anguish.

She couldn't help herself. With her heart aching for him, she reached over and touched his cheek. Instead of pulling away, he leaned against her palm.

"She's starting to look just like Mandy, Tara. I can't...I can't bear to look at my own child anymore."

Oh, her poor love. He was such a good person and this was tying him in knots, turning him into something he had always hated. "Maybe you should tell me about the night Chloe was born. Tell me what really happened."

Cam gave in and closed his eyes, wearily leaning his head against the couch cushions. "Mandy had been having a difficult pregnancy and needed bed rest and complete quiet. At the eighth month, we were both holding our breaths, waiting for the emergency we feared was coming."

He cleared his throat but kept his eyes closed against the terrible images running in his head. Did he have the courage to tell this tale to Tara?

Yes. But only to Tara, and he'd only just realized that. "I knew her life was in danger, but when she encouraged me to continue with my job like nothing was wrong, I didn't argue. There wasn't anything I could do to help her. It was so frustrating sitting around and watching the hours tick by.

"So when our office needed to transport a prisoner on Christmas Eve day to stand trial in Denver, I volunteered so the deputies could stay with their families. I figured nothing would happen to Mandy on Christmas Eve, anyway. She'd been feeling a little better and her parents had arrived to be with her after the baby came. I knew they planned a big get-together up here for the holiday. They were due for dinner in a few hours. I kept telling myself nothing could go very wrong in just an afternoon."

"But it did, didn't it?" Tara's voice was soft. Comforting.

He didn't deserve her sympathy—didn't want it. "I was too lost in my head, worrying about Mandy and the baby coming. Not paying close enough attention to my surroundings." He swallowed down the curse he usually spat out over his own stupidity.

He was used to shouldering the blame silently, but Tara needed to hear all of it. She needed to really understand what a bastard he was.

"At a rest stop, the prisoner's buddies attacked my sheriff's cruiser. Before I knew what hit me, my prisoner was escaping and I was being roughed up and left for dead by his two pals."

"Oh, Cam. That's not what I thought you would say at all. I'm so sorry. Is that how you hurt your knee?"

"How'd you know…?" In the past, Tara had always known everything about how he was doing—both physically and emotionally—they'd had that kind of connection without saying a word. "Mandy's parents kept the truth out of the papers, trying to save my law enforcement career. But the assault left me with a broken kneecap and two shots in the head. I was in a coma for six weeks. Near death for a while. When I got out, I had to take disability leave. Actually, I was ashamed to face the world after making such a huge mistake. And worse, my wife was…already buried."

Tara took his hand in her own. "You don't have to finish this."

"Yeah, I think I do." There was a time when Tara's enchanting voice and sweet way alternately soothed and stirred him. Now, it scraped at his memories and left him raw.

"If it wasn't for my careless inattention—" He swallowed his hurt and went on. "You see, after someone called Mandy and told her I was in the hospital and close to dying, she panicked. Ran to her car and started down the mountain to come for me. Her parents found her on their way up an hour later, still in her car, bleeding and unconscious. The doctors delivered Chloe just as Mandy took her last breath."

Tara's cheeks were wet, her eyes still full of tears. "Cam… that wasn't your fault. You did nothing—"

"Stop it." He pulled his hand away. "You sound like Mandy's parents. But I know the truth." She was making him out to be a hero and a good husband, but he'd never been either one.

And no one else, especially Tara, would ever know all of it. The real reason he hated himself and was beginning to hate his innocent daughter. The truth of what kind of bastard he really was.

Feeling the frustration, the heat, the pain of his guilt, Cam tried to shake some sense into Tara. He gripped her shoulders and shook her hard.

"Open your eyes, Tara. See what's…" The look on her face. The love in her eyes. The understanding. It choked the words right out of his mouth and blurred his vision.

He didn't want her understanding or her sympathy. He wanted her back out of his life, but the conflict was killing him.

Lowering his head, he took her mouth with a fierce kiss. It wasn't at all the same as the tender kisses of their early years. And he didn't put his heart and soul into it the way he had always dreamed their first kiss after so many years would be. Oh no, not hardly.

Instead, he punished her mouth. Punished her for not being his wife, the way they'd always planned. Punished her for letting his parents destroy everything good they'd once had. Punished her for coming back into his life and making him feel alive again.

* * *

Shocked by Cam's surprise assault, Tara gave as good as she got. This wasn't the kiss of a heartsick, grieving man. No, his kiss was wild, desperate—exactly as she had been feeling. A little wild. A lot desperate.

Grabbing hold of the front of his shirt with both hands, she held on while the storm inside him battled at her senses. She had loved this man since she was seven years old. She would not back away from him when he needed her most.

Her heart hurt for him. Hurt for both of them. As much as she needed him physically, her heart was breaking over not being able to make his pain go away.

Tara's cheeks were drenched in tears. Tears she hadn't let herself cry in years. So many tears now. Too many. In a moment she realized half these tears belonged to Cam. But that idea made her cry all the harder.

Cam suddenly broke the kiss and shook her by the shoulders again. "Damn you, Tara. I want you so badly, I can hardly breathe. Damn you. Damn…"

"Love me, Cam. Make love to me the way it used to be. I need you. And you need…"

She couldn't see him clearly through her tears. And words were becoming impossible. Every minute of regret and longing was falling from her eyes like a sudden rainstorm.

Want me back, my love.

"I can't. Won't. You ask too much, dammit." Cam grabbed her up close to his chest, and held her tightly inside his embrace so she couldn't see his face.

She cried, now harder than ever, for their lost years and the gulf between them. For the relationship that would never be repaired. Tara exhausted herself crying against his shoulder, as nothing else in the world—not a lonely little girl needing help—not a hitman waiting for his kill—could keep her mind from falling into the deep blackness of their empty past and bleak future.

When she finally grew cold, she opened her eyes. And found

herself alone. A creeping gray dawn blocked the windows, and the fireplace was dark and cheerless.

Where was Cam? Was it morning? Had they slept all night holding on to each other?

She restarted the fire and then went to search for him. The door alarms were still armed and she doubted he had gone out to the animals. So where…?

A sound on the front porch poured a shot of cold fear through her still-sleepy veins. She dived back into the great room for her backpack and rescued her weapon from the inside pocket. Maybe the hitman had found a way through the mountain of snow.

But when she chanced a look out to the porch, nothing was there but ice and beyond that the blizzard, still raging. Then she heard the noise again and this time saw a shower of snow coming from the roof and mixing with the swirling, windblown flakes.

Cam. Cleaning off the porch roof? Of course. Who else?

Tara put away her .38, dashed into the kitchen and started a pot of coffee, then made her way to the front bedroom upstairs. She spotted Cam's silhouette through the frosty window as he wielded a snow shovel and balanced on the roof of the front porch. There was nothing she could do to help.

Sighing and suddenly starving, she started back down to the kitchen. When she hit the bottom of the stairs, the depressing atmosphere of the house suddenly began to prey on her nerves. How many more days would she be stuck here with a man who refused to give her a real chance? A man who even refused to have Christmas, for pity's sake?

Cam had always loved the holiday season, just like she did. How could he deny himself, deny his daughter, the joy of Christmas in their wonderful home? Especially over guilt for something that was not his fault.

Well, she would not deny herself. No way.

If she was stuck here, and couldn't have Cam, she would at least have Christmas.

* * *

After Cam warmed up over a breakfast of the oatmeal Tara had fixed while he was on the roof, he excused himself and went to feed the animals. Breakfast had been a desolate affair and he was happy for the excuse to leave and get out of the chilly atmosphere of the warm kitchen.

He knew Tara was as miserable as he was, but he refused to talk about it with her anymore. Last night when she'd begged him to make love to her, and he'd needed her so badly he thought death might be the preferable way out, everything suddenly became clear.

He was ashamed of what he'd become and what had brought him to it. He could barely face Tara now, knowing the truth. She hadn't taken his parents' money. But the guilt of what *he'd* been still haunted him.

Stomping back into the kitchen, he was ready to confront her. To tell her to keep her distance while they were forced into this close proximity. He didn't care if she understood his reasons or not. No questions. He would find a quiet place upstairs to be alone while she stayed downstairs on her own.

As he searched her out to tell her his new plan and couldn't find her, he worked up a good steam of mad. He hadn't asked for this. She'd interrupted his life, not the other way around. He wouldn't force her to leave, but he'd only let her stay until they could reach the sheriff. After that, she could go. Out of his life again, the same way she went before.

Yes, he still loved her and wanted her. But that was the whole problem. By the time he realized the door to the attic stairs was standing open, he was all geared up for an argument. Storming up the stairs, Cam rounded the last corner with his fists tight, ready to pick a fight so he wouldn't be tempted.

The sight that greeted him punched him smack in the gut. Tara was sitting on his grandmother's antique chaise longue, holding a box of Christmas ornaments on her lap. She looked so—so much like family, it stopped him cold.

"What the hell do you think you're doing?"

"Remember these?" She held out two of the handmade tree ornaments they'd once made together.

"Stop it, Tara. I don't want to remember." It hurt too much. "Put that junk away and…"

He grabbed her by the wrist, and something in his mind just snapped.

Chapter 5

Cam was pissed. She had no right to drag out old memories and wave them in his face. Neither one of them was the same person as when they'd made those ornaments.

Glaring at her, he suddenly experienced swamping waves of lust and deep need, washing over him like the winter winds over the mountaintops. Past melted into present, and the lost years crumbled to dust.

"You're not the same sweet girl I knew," he said through gritted teeth.

"I'm not sweet—or soft. Not anymore. You've changed, too. But every time I look at you I still hear music."

"Stop that!" She had to stop.

"You're angry? At me?"

"I'm mad as hell at you. At me, too." He jerked her up and ornaments went flying. "I don't want to need you this much."

Dragging her lush body against him and pulling her bottom against the hard ridge of his erection, he let her experience the truth of what he was feeling. "I hate you for coming back and making me crazy." He plastered his mouth against hers and backed them against the wall.

"I need you, Cam," she whispered against his lips. Looping her arms around his neck, she flattened her breasts to his chest. "You need me."

Blinded by furious desire, he ripped her T-shirt up and over her head. "I don't…I don't…"

She stood naked to the waist, gazing at him, and he was lost. Taking one of her peaked nipples into his mouth, Cam plundered her with caresses. He let his hands roam over familiar territory as they willed. He allowed the wild man inside him to come out of his dreams.

He stopped touching her only long enough to release his zipper. Even with his eyes locked on her face, he knew Tara was wiggling out of her jeans. This was crazy. They shouldn't—he didn't own any condoms and couldn't have stopped long enough if he did. So help him, he couldn't bring himself to let her go for one second. Not now that he had her this close.

Completely naked now, she began climbing his legs in a frantic effort to wrap her long limbs around his thighs. As she sidled closer, his bad knee buckled. He twirled them both around so he could brace her back against the wall.

This was his Tara in the flesh. His. At last.

She locked her legs around his waist and he reached between them to position his erection to her wet opening. God, the heat between them was incredible. He let the fiery flames engulf him.

"Now," he groaned. "Nothing matters but now."

He flexed and plunged while she sucked in a breath. "That's so good." She bit into his shoulder and hung on as he buried himself deeper in her tight heat.

Consumed by this, whatever this was, he plied her with whispered kisses. It felt like heaven—and it felt like hell.

He didn't just want sex with her—he wanted to claim his right. She was his first. Would always be his. She'd dominated his mind and his dreams for most of his life.

As she rocked frantically against him, his body became one

raw bundle of electricity. He caught her gasps with his kisses until she finally stiffened in his arms and gave a keening cry. He felt the shock waves rolling through her body and pulling him in. Her orgasm was powerful, beautiful. It took him over the edge along with her. His life seemed right for the first time in years.

"I love you," she groaned. "I've never stopped loving you."

Her words were like a bucket of frigid water over his head, bringing him back to reality. Groping for balance against the wall, he held her steady until his body stopped quaking and his mind cleared from the blast of fireworks.

He'd just been through possibly the most all-consuming experience of his entire life. And it was the worst thing that could've happened. He wanted to do it again and again.

Hell. His determination and resolve had been completely and utterly undone by his own foolhardiness. Now what?

Tara felt the change come over Cam like a cold shower. Before he'd even moved or said a word.

"Better get dressed," he whispered. "The generator's kicked off again."

That was it? Those were the only words he could spare for her? After she'd given her all and confessed her love.

She felt foolish for expecting words of undying love. But she would've done fine with a single line about how he hoped she was okay and how great they were together. She was okay. More than okay. She felt changed. Whole again.

When he released her and let her ease down the wall to her feet, Tara caught a glimpse of his eyes. The same wonder and fear that she was feeling showed right in his eyes before he averted them and shut her out again.

He felt as scared as she did. She was petrified. Making love with Cam again had been a life-changing rush. Slightly scary and over the top. She didn't want whatever they had reignited to be over, but knew it must end soon, anyway. She didn't really belong here.

She turned and pulled on her T-shirt, but was determined not let him entirely escape into his shell again. Not now.

"Let's go to the great room and talk," she suggested.

Cam shook his head while he finished zipping up, but then said, "I'll add a few logs to the fire, and I want to try calling out again."

What had happened between them was more than sex. She knew it and felt sure he did, too. She slipped into her jeans, but left off the panties.

Cam stood at the doorway, his sandy-brown hair all messed and his shirt hanging out of his belt, waiting for her. The man was just too delicious. She wanted to reach out to him again, but held back for the moment.

Something else needed to be said first. "Please let me put up these decorations. There's only a couple of days left until Christmas, and I think we need a little good cheer."

His expression became a complex puzzle of emotions as he thought it over. "All right. But downstairs only. And not many. You can pack them away again before you leave."

Well, it was a start. A crack in the icy wall he'd erected between them. When he turned his back, Tara hurried to gather everything into the box, muttering about the Grinch under her breath. He probably didn't want to touch her again, either. But she would have something to say about both of those things.

As the sun dipped low behind Mt. Lincoln Peak much later that afternoon, Cam found himself wondering where the hell Tara had gone. He'd spent the whole day avoiding her, though it had been tough. Her Christmas carol-singing had filled the entire house with lively sounds—the noise of a happy woman working that hadn't been heard inside these walls in over four years. The lilting sounds had made his heart sing and he nearly forgot why he'd done without for so long.

His damned mind kept betraying him. Replaying the look on her face right before he'd coldly told her to get dressed. Once upon a time he'd thrilled to see that same expression on her face. Love. He remembered it clearly. The day he'd asked her to marry him.

He knew that look promised happy endings. But it had all been a lie back then. And now, even if it were suddenly to come true, he didn't deserve anyone's love and would prefer to hide from the responsibility of telling her as much.

What was he to tell her, anyway? That he loved her too? That he'd never stopped—not for one moment? He couldn't face the guilt. It shamed him to think what a bastard he'd been to marry someone else when his heart had always belonged to Tara.

After checking every room in the house and finding them all empty, Cam finally checked the coat closet and then the kitchen door. Tara's coat was missing and the door alarm had been reset. He groaned. She couldn't simply go off like this when a killer was after her, and he intended to tell her so.

He grabbed his coat and boots and wished for once that he'd kept one of his grandfather's guns in the house for emergencies, but he'd gotten rid of them after bringing Chloe home. What if Tara was in trouble? Already in the hands of her stalker?

The minute Cam hit the back porch, he realized the brunt of the storm was past. Late-afternoon sunshine peeked through the gray. He heard a disturbance coming from the direction of the stand of evergreens behind the barn.

Glancing over his shoulder at the firewood chopping block, he noted that Jim's ax was missing. Storming through the deep snow, following her footsteps, Cam rounded the barn and spotted Tara. Sure enough, she was trying to bring down one of the smaller trees.

His tree. She planned to cut one of the trees from the stand of spruce they'd planted together over twenty years ago. He didn't want the scent of evergreen in his house. Didn't want to remember anything more about their past life than he already did.

But as he came closer, the sight of that flushed face and those blue eyes of hers all lit up with enthusiasm and determination stopped him cold. He couldn't breathe for a moment. And when he did suck in a deep breath, his lungs filled with frigid air. Cam gasped involuntarily.

Tara turned to him, the expression on her face daring him to try stopping her. "What?" she finally said.

"Just look at you." It was all he could manage.

She frowned and put her hand on her hip in defiance. "Yes, it's me, chopping down one of your trees. I want a Christmas whether you want one or not. I'm not going to spend…"

He barked out a laugh, surprising both of them. "You look beautiful. Exactly the way you looked as a kid planting this stand. I don't think you've aged a day."

Tara blushed and pushed a flyaway strand of hair behind her ear. "Thanks, I guess." She gave him a tentative smile. "So you don't mind…about the tree coming in?"

"No." Suddenly he didn't. Suddenly it felt as if his mind was clearing along with the clouds. "Let me help you."

She stood, shaking her head. "What about your knee?"

"It's fine. I'm not crippled, it just aches sometimes in the cold." He reached for the ax.

Shrugging, she handed it over. "If your knee isn't the problem, then why haven't you gone back to work?"

Gritting his teeth as he planted the ax blade in the wood, he ground out, "I knew you wouldn't let the wounds alone. You'll just have to pick at them until they open up again, won't you?"

"I only want to understand." She grabbed the top of the tree as it leaned in her direction.

"Fine. Let's move inside and we can talk."

But they didn't talk. Not about the things that mattered the most to Tara. Oh, they argued plenty. About where the tree should go. About putting lights on a tree with minimal electricity available to turn them on. They argued about everything, including which decorations would go best on the medium-size tree.

This wasn't like the Cam she remembered. The man she remembered gave the people around him every single thing they requested. He was the good boy who grew into the good man who wanted to please the world. But somehow that giving boy was gone and in his place was this man with hurt in his eyes.

Much later that evening, as the fire blazed at their backs and Cam steadied the shaky stepladder beneath her, he handed her a different possibility to try at the top. "Didn't your grandmother used to have an angel she liked to use as a topper?"

"I don't want an angel," he mumbled. "Try one of these stars or a nutcracker."

She held up the five-pointed glass star he'd handed her. "Nope. This one looks best with lights behind it. Hand me another. Why don't you want an angel?"

"Chloe."

Tara tried a silver star. "Your daughter? Doesn't she like angels?" When he didn't answer right away, she added, "Why aren't the two of you together for the holidays?"

After another long pause, Cam said, "Things haven't been the best between Chloe and me lately. We were fine while she was a baby, but now that she's talking and needing more than…I…I…"

Tara turned to look down at him. "What? She's still a baby. What could she possibly have done to…?"

Cam's expression was stricken, full of pain. "I look at her and see everything that could've been. Every mistake I've made is written in her eyes. It breaks my heart. It's not her fault. None of it. But someday she'll know what a bastard her father really is. I just want her to disappear and take my memories along with her."

"Oh, Cam." She reached out for him, but he turned away.

Tara shifted, trying to bring him back. Then the ladder collapsed under her.

Instinctively Cam spun at the sound behind his back and caught Tara right before she would've hit the ground. With his heart pounding in his chest and his breathing labored, he carried her over to the sofa and sat down with her still in his arms.

"Thanks," she breathed. She gazed up at him through the firelight.

He took in the sight of her. Her hair had frizzed up in burnt-red ringlets. She wore no makeup but her lips were the color of rosé wine. Her aqua-colored eyes still carried the deep-purple smudges of exhaustion underneath, but they glittered in the light of the fire. Tara had never been pretty. Not in the classical sense like Mandy's sophisticated looks. But she'd always been fascinating to look at, full of color and brimming with life. Holding her was like capturing a firefly in his hands.

If she'd broken her neck in a fall, it would've been all his fault. He closed his eyes for a moment and tried to steady his nerves.

Visions danced in his head. Visions of the two of them as lovers. He remembered how responsive she had always been to his touch. How well they fit together. He hungered to slowly explore her once again.

She shifted to crawl into his lap. If they spent the next few hours reminiscing and having reunion sex, what or who would it hurt? Maybe he could keep his mind blank—for a while longer. Maybe releasing the tension would stop this yearning to keep her with him always.

When he opened his eyes, she gazed up at him as the sensual awareness grew. "Tara, I have nothing to give but a few old memories. I've become an empty shell and the holidays are particularly tough. But I can't help myself, I want you. I want you naked underneath me—like it used to be."

She reached up and touched his cheek. "I've wanted you forever, my love. We can pretend the last ten years never happened if that's what you want. I'll take whatever you give."

He gave in to the urgent need pounding through his veins and took her mouth. This time he vowed to go slow, to savor every moment. This time he would revel in the texture of her lips. The way her tongue slid seductively over his. She tasted like popcorn and hot chocolate—and like the best part of his past.

When she moaned into his mouth, her need echoed inside him. He shifted her again across his lap so that his erection rubbed against her bottom. She reached for his shirt buttons and he slid his hand up under her shirt. Finding bare skin, a shocking stream of adrenaline coursed through him as he completely lost touch with reality.

Somehow they ended up naked on the rug in front of the fire. His mouth trailed a blaze of hot kisses over her tight nipples and lower—along her abdomen and lower still. She arched upward as he tested her hot spot and found her wet and ready. As he twisted, lowering his mouth and kissing her intimately, he felt her whole body shudder. He used his tongue to bring her to climax. The sounds she made were better than any music to his ears.

When she boldly took him in her mouth in return, he groaned and pulled her up his body. "I wanted this to be slow torture. Keep it up and everything will be over too soon."

She smiled up at him and licked her lips. That was it for him. He grabbed her wrists with one hand and, holding them above her head, he slipped inside her tight warmth.

Home. It was perfect. As in his dreams of her. Tara had always been everything to him.

He watched her eyes, saw the raw, primitive need reflected there, matching his own. They began a familiar rhythm. Matching each other perfectly until they crashed over that waiting edge together.

He leaned his forehead against hers and sighed. "Okay," he said breathlessly. Both a question and a statement.

"Okay," she replied.

And suddenly everything was very, very okay.

They eventually made it upstairs to Cam's bedroom where they made love and dozed, whispering and reminiscing for hours on end. When Tara opened her eyes to the lavender light of early morning, she reached out for him but found his side of the bed had grown cold.

Thinking he may have gone out to feed the animals, Tara

scrambled around and found her clothes. It was Christmas Eve morning and she needed to check on how he was doing in the cold light of his most dreaded day.

Hearing noises in the attic, she went up to check there first. She found him sitting on the chaise, rubbing an antique hobbyhorse with a bottle of wood oil and a rag in his hand. She came up behind him and gently touched his shoulder. He didn't turn but laid his hand over hers—a simple, warm gesture that made her heart flutter.

"It's Chloe's birthday." Cam reared back and checked his handiwork. "This belonged to my grandfather originally. Think she'll like it? She wants a real pony, but she's a little young yet."

"She'll love it," Tara told him as tears swam in her eyes.

Cam turned then to look up at her. "I miss her, Tara. I want to bring her home. Everything has changed."

Thank God. The first morning rays peeked through the dusty window, lighting up the room and brightening Cam's face. "Maybe we'll be able to get through the pass today or tomorrow. I want you to meet Chloe."

Tara felt her heart contract, leaving empty space in her chest where it had just been so full of love. "I would love to meet your daughter." Though there wasn't much of a chance of that. "But the minute the pass opens I'll have to contact the sheriff. I must deliver that thumb drive to the governor immediately and get it out of my possession. Do you think my car is in good enough shape for me to drive out of the woods?"

"I'll drive you where you need to go." Cam stood and took her into his arms. "Now that we've found each other again, I don't want to let you out of my sight."

He kissed her with amazing tenderness and what she could only describe as love. "You've given me a chance to get my life back." Whispering in her ear, he held her close. "I don't know if I can ever get fully past what happened—what I did or didn't do. But you've made me want to try, Tara. Thank you."

She bit down on her lip, not willing to say what was necessary. Not willing to put a stop to the dream.

But as she pulled out of his arms, she saw terror entering his eyes, anyway. "What's wrong, honey? What…?"

From not far away, a phone rang. "The phones are working!"

The two of them raced down the stairs and found the nearest landline phone. The caller was the sheriff, telling Cam the pass had been open for several hours. As Cam explained about her presence and that he wanted the sheriff to come up and hear her story, Tara zipped downstairs and retrieved her cell. Within minutes she'd reached the governor on his private line. After a moment's negotiation, they decided to meet at the local sheriff's office rather than take any more chances. The governor would contact the FBI and then leave for Juniper immediately.

Cam started down the stairs as her call was ending. "I heard your end. The sheriff's on his way up here, but I can call him back if you want. Do you have everything ready to leave?"

She turned and opened her mouth to answer, but never got the chance.

"Good question, Miss Jackson." A tall, thin stranger stood in the hallway with a nine-millimeter Walther P5 pointed directly at her head. "Come down the stairs, Mr. Farrell. I'd like to hear the answer to your question, too."

The hitman was already in the house. It was too late to run and Cam was in the middle of her fight. *Oh, Cam.*

Chapter 6

Tara. Cam gritted his teeth as he slowly came down the stairs toward the bastard who held a gun on the woman he loved. He halted at the bottom of the stairs and waited for the hitman to flinch. All he needed was one slipup. One blink and he'd have the guy.

"Stay where you are," the hitman ordered. "Now then…" He inched closer to Tara and grabbed her by the shoulder, pulling her up next to his body. "Ms. Jackson here is going to tell us where she put that computer chip. And then, Mr. Farrell, you are going to retrieve it."

"No, Cam. He'll kill you the minute you have it in your hand."

"Shut up." The hitman put her in a neck lock and pushed the tip of his weapon into her temple. "I don't have a lot of time to spare. Tell me now or I'll kill him first."

Cam fisted and opened his hands, bouncing lightly on the balls of his feet. This bastard was asking for it.

Tara's face was red, her eyes wide in fear. "All right. All right. Don't hurt him."

The man flashed the gun toward Cam then back to Tara's nose. "Where, dammit?"

"It's in my backpack, Cam. In a hidden pocket at the very bottom."

"Where's the pack?" The hitman sounded harried. "Now!"

"Right here, next to the fireplace." Cam could see Tara was starting to lose consciousness so he moved toward the pack as fast as he dared. "Ease up on her, will you?"

"You find that drive, Farrell. Show it to me. And you'd better be fast and careful."

The gunman's attention was riveted on his moves. Cam hoisted the heavy pack in his arms and with one hand began rifling through it, heading for the bottom. But Cam's fingers touched something else first. Something metallic, solid—and familiar. *Thank you, my love.*

"I think I found it," he said as he slipped his finger through the trigger.

Just then Tara's whole body went limp and the hitman was forced to rearrange his hold on her. He took his eyes off of Cam for the moment. It was all the advantage Cam needed.

Cam pulled the .38 out of the pack, aimed and fired before the hitman had a chance to look his way. Cam had been aiming for his head, many inches above Tara's, but the man was moving and all Cam caught was his shoulder. Fortunately the bullet shot through the hitman's gun arm. The man dropped his weapon and loosened his hold on Tara.

Before Cam could take a step in their direction, Tara came alive, spun and flung the man over her shoulder, pinning him to the ground. The hitman screamed in pain.

"You're still the best shot at ten paces I've ever known, Cam Farrell." She was cracking jokes when he could barely breathe? No doubt her attempt to diffuse the tension. He knew then for sure that he was destined to be with her always. He was helpless to do anything but love her.

* * *

Hours later, Cam waited for Tara and paced through the halls of the sheriff's office. A place he knew well, but no longer felt he belonged. It was not his place.

Tara appeared from behind the closed door to one of the conference rooms. "Why are you still here? Haven't you finished giving your statement? It's Christmas Eve, Cam, go find Chloe."

"I was waiting for you. I'll drive you to wherever you need to go."

She looked up at him, love clearly shining in her eyes. "The governor and I have to go to Denver with the FBI agents who arrived hours ago. The paramedics patched up the hitman and he's in the process of making a statement. I think he's ready to make a deal to testify against the attorney general for a reduced sentence."

Tara took his hands and pulled him to one of the plastic chairs in an alcove. "I can't thank you enough for everything. You saved my life and you…gave me the best few days I've ever had."

Cam didn't like the sound of that. Was she telling him goodbye?

She looked down at their joined hands. "Sheriff Reiner has been really terrific through all of this. Have you thought of someday running against him and going back to work as the sheriff?"

"Reiner is a much better sheriff than I'd ever be. He wouldn't lose his focus at the worst possible moment."

"Cam, nobody blames you for being ambushed. It could've happened to anyone. You need to do what's right for you."

Cam rubbed at the pain developing in his chest. "The only thing I miss about being sheriff is the opportunity to accomplish something worthwhile for the people who voted me into office." He shook his head, not able to consider any kind of future without Tara. Now that he'd found her again, he wasn't giving her a chance to get away.

"Then run for another office." She gazed up at him with

those sincere blue eyes and his heart fractured a little more. "You're a born politician and you know it."

"I don't want…" His voice cracked and he was forced to swallow the lump building in his throat. "I don't want to run for anything unless you're with me. You worked in the attorney general's political office, even if it was only a cover. You must have learned a lot. Politicians do better when they have loving spouses.

"And Tara, I lov—"

She jumped up and cut him off. "Don't." Turning her back, she kept speaking softly. "Nothing has changed between us in the last ten years. Not really. We're still—"

He stood as well and cut her off. Taking her in his arms, he pulled her back against his chest so he could whisper in her ear.

"True, I still love you. That hasn't changed. Are you still disappointed in me because I believed my parents' lies? I'm so sorry. Sorry for all of us. But I'm trying to make amends—both to you and to Chloe. I owe you both so much. Please give me a chance."

He heard the sob gurgling out of her chest, but when she spoke, her voice was steady. "You still don't understand. Back then I—never mind. It can't happen, Cam. We're still the same people we always were."

She pulled out of his arms and turned, a bruised look in her eyes and tears staining her cheeks. "I'm the one who's sorry. I'm glad you're going to make a new life for yourself and your daughter. Really. But it can't be with me. I apologize if I seemed to be leading you on."

Spinning again with her chin held high, she walked purposefully down the hall. "Have a good life, Cam. You deserve it."

"Tara! Come home with me. I can't do this without you." His words echoed in the empty hallway as Tara slipped around a corner and disappeared without a goodbye.

Stricken with pain and ready to explode in frustration, Cam

fisted his hands, clenched his teeth and stormed out of the sheriff's offices. He'd loved her all his life. How could he ever be anything without Tara?

Tara unlocked her basic one-bedroom apartment in Denver and slipped inside. This was one Christmas Day she was glad to finally see coming to an end. Only a few more hours left and then she could put a period on this whole crazy holiday.

Without turning on the lights, she went to the windows, closed the blinds and drew the blackout curtains. When she felt it was safe, she turned on the night-light over the stove. Not that there was much for anyone to see within these cold and lonely rooms. She'd only ever used this space to sleep and shower. It might as well have been a motel room for all the use she'd ever made of what she laughingly referred to as home.

But the governor and the FBI had convinced her that she was still at risk, that as long as the attorney general was at large, and perhaps even after he was captured, her life would remain on the line. She would have to move. Go into temporary hiding, maybe even change her name, at least until his trial.

The FBI had suggested using the U.S. Marshals Service Witness Protection program, but she'd declined the offer. No need. She could protect herself just fine and there wasn't anyone who would miss her if she suddenly disappeared. Nothing to hold her here.

Her father was in prison—for good this time. Not that it mattered. He hadn't acknowledged her existence since she'd been a kid. And her mother moved to the Canadian Rockies years ago. For a split second, Tara thought of joining her up there. But then she remembered that a couple of years back her mother had found a new husband and had a whole litter of young stepchildren to raise. Uh-uh. That would be no place for her now.

Shrugging, Tara began cleaning out her fridge, though it contained little but leftovers and a carton of out-of-date milk. She was used to not having a real home. There'd only been that one time in her whole life when she'd ever felt wanted enough to really settle in—at Cam's grandparents' house.

The thought of his home threatened to release the tears that had stayed right below the surface for the last twenty-four hours since she'd told Cam goodbye. But she never belonged in his world. Not really. She was still the girl from the wrong side of town. She bit her lip to stop it from trembling and twist-tied the garbage bag she'd filled.

Love was for fools. Just look at what it had done for her mother. Tara would put Cam's memory back in the tidy little spot in her heart where she'd been keeping it for all these years. Better for everyone that way.

Ten years ago she'd grown tougher after learning that even love was not enough sometimes. She could do it again.

Making her way to the closet in the dark, she flipped her one suitcase onto the bed and began cramming it with the two business suits and four pairs of jeans she owned. The nightstand drawer full of underwear and nightgowns came next. After that, Tara looked around and decided she could easily call the furniture rental place in the morning and tell them to pick up the rest of their stuff.

Not much to show for a whole life.

Rolling her bag behind her, she made her way back to the kitchen to pick up the garbage and turn out the light. She'd already been in the apartment for too long.

As she rounded the corner, she noticed her one landline phone. Better disconnect it and take it with her. But then she saw the answering machine blinking. Messages?

Thinking a caller might've been the attorney general's lawyer ready to make some kind of deal, she hit the button. The voice that came through the speaker was right out of her dreams.

"Tara, are you okay? I'm worried about you. Merry Christmas, honey." Cam's voice was none too steady.

She knew how he felt. Her own legs started shaking under her at the mere sound of his voice. That's why she'd refused to take his calls to her cell. She held on to the kitchen counter and listened to the rest of his message.

"You can't leave things this way, Tara. It isn't fair. Don't I deserve a better explanation of what's wrong? At least call me and let me know that you're alive and well. Please consider meeting with me. Talk to me. Come home."

For seconds after he'd hung up she just stared at the silent phone, shell-shocked and numb. But a few of his words kept repeating and repeating in her mind.

"Don't I deserve…? Home…"

Cam threw down the dish towel at the sound of the doorbell, wondering who it could be at this hour. His in-laws had left a couple of hours ago and Chloe was tucked away and fast asleep in her bed. A birthday party at her grandparents' and a big Christmas morning at home had tuckered his little charmer out.

At nearly midnight, Cam couldn't imagine who would risk the still-slick mountain roads to come to his door. The sheriff? Alarmed by the idea of bad news, Cam checked out the window and saw a familiar shape before he disengaged the security and opened the front door.

"Tara!" He dragged her into his arms. "Why didn't you call? How did you get here?"

She gazed up at him. "Can I come in and talk?" The love was still in her eyes, but so was a mountain of hesitation.

Quietly he settled her at the kitchen table and made them a pot of coffee. He was determined not to let her out of his sight again. No matter what she had to say. But as he waited, his heart thumped wildly in his chest.

"The FBI loaned me an unmarked car. I have to stay out of sight for a while." She looked down into her mug. "I've decided you were right, Cam. I do owe you an explanation. You shouldn't have to go on with your life still guessing. That isn't fair.

"By the way, did you at least see your daughter on her birthday? Give her the rocking horse?"

He wanted to reach out to her, but fisted his hands around his mug instead. "Chloe is upstairs in her bed. Where she belongs. She loved the horse but made me promise next year it would be a real pony."

Tara exhaled. "Good. That's good."

"Tara, honey…"

She shook her head. "Let me just say this, please. Ten years ago when your parents lied to you about me, I could have proved them wrong right then. I had the scholarship letters that I could have shown you. But I decided the best thing for you was for us to break up—so I stayed silent."

Cam held his breath, unable to speak.

She shook her head. "I didn't tell you because it was better for your future. You were born to be a politician. You're going to run for a major office someday, Cam. I've always known that. And I also knew that who I am, where I come from, could not help you. In fact, my background would only be a hindrance to your career.

"It still would be," she said with a sigh. "My father is a convicted career criminal and a murderer. My mother cleaned hotel rooms for a living. Wouldn't your political rivals just love to use that against you?"

"That's it? You're saying you believed all the crap my mother used to spout about you not being good enough? How could you claim to love me and not know me any better than that?" Cam stood, pushed back his chair and pulled her into his arms—though she was still fighting him.

"Listen to me. I. Love. You. When you and I marry, that will make me and Chloe your only family. Who cares about people who are related to you just by biology? Anyone who dares to make a public fuss about your past family will have to deal with me. And I suspect the voters would be on our side of that argument. If they weren't on our side—well, their political office wouldn't be worth having. Not without you."

"When we marry? Cam, no. I…"

Suddenly panicked that she would still walk away, Cam

fought for calm. "Did you lie when you said you loved me? Did you?"

Shaking her head, she murmured, "I have loved you all my life. But that doesn't mean—"

Cam couldn't let her finish. Not without showing her the truth of what he felt. He kissed her. The kiss of a man still desperately in love—as he had also been all of his life.

"Don't leave me again," he whispered against her mouth. "Stay with me. Make me whole."

"Daddy?" A little voice called from behind him. "I'm thirsty. What's going on?"

"Chloe." Cam turned his head to see his sleepy daughter standing just inside the kitchen with her teddy under one arm. "You should be asleep, baby. But now that you're up, I want you to meet…"

"My angel! Daddy, you found her for me." Chloe came closer and looked up at Tara with a serious expression on her sweet face. "I'm Chloe. I know you. You're going to be my new mommy.

"Right, Daddy?"

Cam turned to Tara, holding his breath. Tara's eyes filled with tears as she smiled down at his child and then gazed up at him.

"Two against one. I give up." She turned back to Chloe and held out her hand to bring his baby into the circle of their love. "Yes, honey. I guess I'm going to be your new mommy."

Chloe snuggled close and buried her face in Tara's tummy. "My angel."

Cam wrapped them both in his arms, silently giving thanks to whatever force had really brought Tara back into his life and had given him a second chance. This time he vowed it would be forever.

* * * * *

SAVING CHRISTMAS

Loreth Anne White

For my parents, who married two days before Christmas, forever entwining memories of the season with memories of their love.

Chapter 1

December 22, 1600 Zulu

A thick equatorial stillness hung over the U.S. embassy's residential compound in Kigali, broken only by a sudden shrill screech from a troop of silver-gray monkeys, three of them swinging down through the iroko trees and dropping into an open-walled, thatched lapa where Cass Rousseau, West Africa staff correspondent for CBN International, was setting up to interview Susan Swift, U.S. Deputy Chief of Mission.

Since it was a Sunday, most State Department staff and their families were in the residential compound, which lay in the foothills of jungle-encrusted mountains that reached up into hot, wet mist—and most were lying low in their bungalows, avoiding the energy-sapping heat.

The only reminder that it was just three days before Christmas in this tiny country wedged between Ghana and Cote d'Ivoire was the fake white tree in front of which Swift had positioned her seat for the interview. Decorated with tiny ornaments crafted from African beads, the tree looked incongruous against the verdant backdrop. But even that plastic symbol of the season was too much for Cass. Especially today.

Sweat beaded across her upper lip as she repositioned her fluorescent light stand, trying to stay focused on her job—the fewer prompts that tomorrow was her wedding anniversary, the better.

Christmas had once represented a time of hope and dreams for Cass. Then her son, Jacob, had been killed.

Hope and dreams died with him that day.

So had her marriage.

Now she liked to get as far away as she could from anything even vaguely reminiscent of cool, snow-covered mountains, twinkling lights, the scent of gingerbread, crackling fires, roasting turkeys. Now she preferred chasing stories—the closer the shaves, the sharper the adrenaline, the hotter and more foreign the locale, the better.

However, things had finally grown calm in Kigali since the first democratic elections thirteen months ago. So calm that U.S. Ambassador Jon Wight had taken a month of home leave, his duties falling to Susan Swift in the interim.

This was great for the Kigali people, but not for Cass. The lag in breakneck action gave her time to dwell on the past, to remember. She'd begun to think of moving on.

Opening her backpack, Cass removed a small mirror and checked herself out under the lighting. She dabbed a tissue over her damp brow, freshened her lip gloss.

"Sorry about the lack of air-conditioning," Swift said with a laugh as she watched Cass. "Maybe in another year we'll actually get some—seems we're not a high priority on the department budget."

Cass smiled and snapped the mirror shut. She liked Swift. She liked that a woman was in charge, and she liked that Swift had a sense of humor. "Believe me, I've dealt with way worse than melting makeup. And I do like to think that viewers cut us beleaguered foreign correspondents some slack in the looks department from time to time." She motioned to her cameraman, Samuel Sekibo, as she spoke. "Ready to roll, Sam?"

He shot a big thumbs-up, his ebony-skinned face splitting into a broad, white grin. "Ready to roll 'em, boss," he said in his resonating bass. Cass repressed a smile. Sam uttered those same words without fail each time—she'd miss them, and him, when she moved on.

Since she'd arrived to cover the country's turbulent transition into a democracy, Cass had made some firm and fast friends among the staff at the local Kigali news station where CBN rented space for her, and where she'd set up her editing equipment.

Sam was one of them. He contracted out to Cass, working as her driver, translator and camera guy. Another was Gillian Tsabatu, a feisty young reporter with blood ties to the Kigali royal family. In addition to challenging viewers with her liberal—and often risqué—reporting, Gillian had become Cass's guide into the complex cultures, religions and tribal fabric of this once volatile country. And she'd become a dear friend in the process.

"And are you ready, Mrs. Swift?"

"Please, call me Susan," the Deputy Chief of Mission said, straightening her skirt. She sat ramrod-straight, her brown hair cropped bluntly at her jaw, exuding a businesslike efficiency and elegance at the same time. A true diplomat, thought Cass as she seated herself in the wicker chair opposite Swift. Her gaze fell unintentionally to Swift's hands, to the simple gold band on her ring finger.

Cass cleared her throat, glanced away quickly. No matter how she tried, this time of year was rough. Talking to this woman about how she juggled both family and job was going to be of no help, either.

She should have found a way to weasel out of this assignment, but with the ambassador away and the political situation in the country deathly calm, Cass had needed to fill airtime. And Swift was a woman on the fast track, pegged for high office, possibly even Secretary of State down the road.

Cass's editors liked the idea of a profile on this very ambitious chargé d'affaires who was also a mother of three—clearly a wife whose husband gave her all the room and support she needed to pursue her career around the world, Cass thought.

Unlike what Jack had given her.

Cass cursed silently. *This* is what happened when the hard news went soft—she was forced to resort to this stuff.

"I'll do a proper introduction in the final edit, but for now we'll jump straight into the questions, if that's okay?"

"Go right ahead."

One of the monkeys perched on the wall nearby watched them with interest as it tore open a wild blood orange, its teeth yellow as it sucked at the fruit. Cass leaned forward slightly. "Madame Swift, it's been just over a year now since Kigali voted for its first president, effectively putting an end to decades of oppressive monarchy-military rule. What has this transition meant to both the people of Kigali and to the United States? And where to from here?"

"Those elections, thanks in part to the forward thinking of King Harold Savungi, have opened doors to this, our first diplomatic mission to Kigali. And Kigali is a country of strategic importance in this region. It has also paved the way for military-to-military contact. For example, earlier this year a Special Forces Operational Detachment from the third Special Forces Group Airborne was tasked to develop a training plan to assist in the development of a new Kigali army. And now that—" Swift was suddenly interrupted by an aide carrying a phone, signaling to her it was urgent.

A frown creased Swift's brow. She turned to Cass. "Can you excuse me a—"

But the aide didn't wait. He came over to Swift's chair, bent over her, lowering his voice, but not enough to escape Cass's hearing. "It's one of the marines," he whispered urgently. "He says the embassy building in Molatu is under attack—the entire capital under siege."

"What?" whispered Swift.

"At 3:00 p.m. about five hundred men wearing red

bandannas or armbands entered the city on technical vehicles, quickly engaging in urban combat with Kigali troops. The parliamentary buildings have been breached, the president and his family are missing and now the U.S. embassy building itself is under attack by revolutionary forces—"

"*What* forces?" The shock on Swift's face was blatant. "We had no warning of this?"

More phones started to ring, additional staff rushing into the lapa. Cass motioned quietly to Samuel to keep rolling video as Swift surged up from her chair. She snatched the receiver from her aide. "This is DCM Swift. I'm putting you on speaker." She pressed a button.

Tension crackled in the sweltering heat as the distant sound of staccato gunfire reached them via speakerphone. The marine yelled over the noise. "The American embassy is under attack! We've taken casualties—the contracted guards outside the gates are all down. Only two of us inside. Crowds are out of control, throwing rocks, smashing windows...a truck is presently ramming the embassy gates. We—" The sound of glass shattering came over the speaker. Someone swore. The line went dead.

Faces, pale, looked at each other.

"Get me the White House!" Swift said.

A sharp thrill ripped through Cass. "Samuel, quick," she whispered. "Hand me our sat phone." Cass moved rapidly across the lapa and down the stairs onto the lawn, dialing the CBN newsroom, heart racing. *This* is the kind of story she lived for.

This would help her endure Christmas, get past her wedding anniversary without having to think of Jack.

Or Jacob.

"I've got breaking news here, Paul," she told the CBN staffer manning the news desk. "U.S. embassy is under attack—looks like a coup attempt by as yet unidentified forces. Most of the U.S. staff are safe at the residential compound, but they've lost contact with the two marines guarding the embassy."

"Where are you?" said Paul.

"I was interviewing Susan Swift when word broke. She's presently on the line with the Joint Chiefs of Staff. Can you get me live sat hookup—I'm going to need to stay on this all night as it develops."

"Hang on a sec, Cass."

She waited for a moment, then shot a thumbs-up to Samuel. "We go live in twenty!"

Monday, December 23, 0038 Zulu

Cass stood on the dark lawn illuminated by her portable fluorescent light stand. Although it was just after midnight, the equatorial night felt thicker, hotter. She could now smell smoke, hear gunfire in the distance.

"The violence that erupted in the capital yesterday has spread rapidly to residential and rural areas during the night," she said into her mic, eyes focused on the camera. "Reports of arson, looting and the random rape and slaughter of innocent civilians were coming in from Molatu before the phone system went down—" Her lighting suddenly dimmed. All the lights in Swift's home died for a moment. Cass hesitated.

A generator kicked in and the lights went on again. She continued. "Cell towers and power grids are also being sabotaged in what appears to be a coordinated attempt by as yet unidentified rebel forces to cut off communication across the entire country. Armed vehicles carrying RPG artillery are now reported to be heading towards the U.S. embassy's residential compound located about twenty miles outside of Molatu. Kigali troops loyal to King Harold Savungi are reported to be in a defensive position at a blockade along the highway, but are taking severe casualties. U.S. Deputy Chief of Mission Susan Swift has now ordered the evacuation of all non-combatant embassy personnel and their families. Swift has personally vowed to stay on as long as she can, but it appears the diplomatic situation is becoming untenable. Earlier this evening, the U.S. Department of Defense mobilized the first available resource in this region, a Special Forces Operational

Detachment Alpha, consisting of twelve men who were in Kigali to develop a training plan for the new army. They will start spearheading the evacuation."

As she spoke, Cass heard the first helicopter thudding in the thick air. "Meanwhile, the *U.S.S. Shackleton,* a naval helicopter ship with twelve hundred marines on board, has been deployed to the area. The ship is expected to arrive within the next twenty-four hours. It will wait off the coast to help with the evacuation of Americans." Cass spoke louder as a Black Hawk descended over the compound. Trees began to whip in the downdraft, leaves and debris flying out over the lawn. Monkeys screamed, scattering down from the iroko trees.

Cass motioned to Sam to get footage of the chopper setting down. Swift stood up on the patio, illuminated by the security spotlights around her home, her hair whipping around her face.

The helo door swung open. Cass signaled quickly for Sam to move in closer for a better shot. A special forces soldier hopped down onto the grass—tall, powerful.

And Cass froze dead in her tracks.

Her entire world stopped spinning as the rotors slowed and the ground felt as though it was falling out from under her.

Jack.

Cass's mouth went bone-dry. A chill breeze blew over her, the sense of snowflakes swirling, icy on her skin…the tiny Colorado church…her special ops soldier coming down the aisle…

The memories came crashing violently, her world narrowing as she recalled the reason they married. Their child.

And the reason they fell apart.

The reason she had not seen, nor spoken to, nor touched Jack in four long years.

He glanced up at Swift, ordered men left and right. Then he turned, and his gaze collided with hers.

Chapter 2

Jack's heart missed a beat. *Cass.* Illuminated by a halo of fluorescent light under a giant flame tree—looking like a translucent angel in a garden of equatorial darkness, and on today, of all days.

Their anniversary.

Relief surged through him. She was here, in the compound, safe, where he could still get her out. And for a moment Jack remained rooted to the spot as he was pounded by an irrational urge to go straight up to her, grab hold of her.

Her mouth opened in shock, her hand holding the mike lowering at her side. And the lost years, the shared memories, seemed to yaw between them, quivering, visceral. Jack's world narrowed—the distant sound of gunfire, the acrid scent of burning villages, fading to just her.

Reflexively his thumb sought the smoothness of the wedding band he still wore, could not give up, and his chest ached with a need he could not define.

He had not seen her in person for four years—although he'd watched her on television. That's how he'd known she was in Kigali.

It's why he was here.

Cass was a like a drug to his system, always had been.

He'd put in for this tour, wanting to be near. So he could protect her, as he hadn't been able to protect his son.

He wanted a second chance.

Because Jack had not given up. Hope was something he still had, even if his wife had none.

An explosion rocked the sky, making the blackness of night glimmer with dull orange light. It snapped him together. Jack swiveled instantly on his heels and made for the DCM Swift, waiting for him atop the slate stairs.

"Madame Swift." He held out his hand as he approached. "Warrant Officer Jack Bannister—"

She took his hand, her skin dry, her grip forceful. "Please, come this way. I've compiled a list of all compound personnel that need to be evacuated. Thankfully most foreign service staff and their families were here at the residence when the rebels attacked."

"Any staff still at the embassy in Molatu?"

"Two marines were inside the building. We lost all contact with them—I fear the worst." Her voice was crisp, her staccato delivery belying the worry he could see in her eyes as she handed him the list. "We've had reports of armed convoys heading this way—the sooner we can evacuate non-combatant staff and their families, the better."

Jack nodded, scanning the list as she spoke. From the look of this list, his team had two hundred and sixteen people to evacuate from this compound within the next few hours.

It was going to be tight. In an emergency, their helos could take twenty passengers. They only had two birds; flights were one hour each way. Mortar fire pounded outside in the hills. Jack glanced up as he felt the vibration, and dust trickled down from the ceiling. Too close for comfort.

He'd seen the devastation from the air. Molatu was burning,

pockets of fire spreading to rural villages. Kigali had descended into complete chaos in mere hours.

Swift inhaled deeply. "In most cases we are aware trouble is brewing, or an army is unhappy, or there's a volcano ready to blow, but…we just did not see this coming. No sign. No murmurs. Nothing. We have no idea who is behind this."

He heard the fear, the self-reproach in her voice.

"No one saw it coming, ma'am. We've been working closely with the Kigali military and we had no warning, either. Don't worry, we'll have everyone out of here and across the border within the next twelve hours. My men are securing the compound perimeter as we speak. We'll commence evacuation protocol with the first Black Hawk. Another is already on its way. We're also working with the Ivory Coast military and expect to use some of their aircraft, which will speed things up. The goal is to get all non-combatant personnel to a safe staging area just inside the Ivoirian border, from where they will be processed and flown out to the *U.S.S. Shackleton* as soon as it arrives."

Swift nodded, jaw tight. "Thank you, Officer."

Jack stepped outside, instinctively searching for Cass. Her name would *not* be on the chargé d'affaires' list. He'd have to find some other way to get her onto that last chopper. He also knew in his gut Cass would resist him.

Monday, December 23, 0122 Zulu

Cass was reporting live via satellite while she still could. She focused on the camera, her audience, delivering her message in her trademark crisp style—but her insides were jelly.

Her anxiety had little to do with the situation on the ground.

It had everything to do with the raw shock of seeing Jack, the way he'd brought the past crashing down around her. Even from a distance she'd felt the electricity in his gaze, the intensity of his wholly consuming focus. Maybe that was what rattled her most—her own reaction to him. She tried to concentrate on her words.

"A twelve-man strong Special Forces Operational Detachment Alpha has just arrived in the U.S. compound to begin the first stage of the evacuation…" But as Cass spoke, she saw Sam reaching for the sat phone in his flak jacket. He kept it on vibrate. It was the newsroom phone and it meant breaking news. Or trouble.

She kept reporting while Sam glanced at the display. He tensed suddenly and took the call. He looked up at Cass, his face tight, and made an abrupt *cut* sign at his neck. Cass's pulse quickened—she'd never seen Sam do this, just quit in the middle of a live segment.

Quickly, she wrapped the broadcast. "This is Cass Rousseau for CBN." She lowered the mic. "That was a live broadcast," she said angrily. "This better be good, Sam."

The whites of his eyes showed fear and his ever-present smile was absent. Sam was huge in stature and with the grim look on his face, he looked a little frightening.

"It's Gillian," he said.

A chill pooled slowly in her gut at the sound of his tone. "What…about Gillian?"

"Boss—" he swallowed, eyes glistening suddenly "—this is serious. We need your help, you must come with me. Now. Or Gillian will die."

From up on the patio, Jack saw Cass touch her cameraman's arm. Their heads were close as they conversed, their movements urgent.

A sense of foreboding curled through him as he watched Cass and her cameraman rapidly packing up their equipment. They headed across the lawn towards the driveway.

Tension rippled through him.

Cass was going to leave the security of the compound?

He glanced over his shoulder at Swift. He could see her through the window, conversing with the Joint Chiefs of Staff via military sat phone.

His orders were to keep her safe, above all else.

You care more about duty to your country than you do about your own family. The words Cass had hurled at him the last time they'd fought stabbed through his brain.

And he swore, once again torn between duty and the woman he loved as he watched his ex disappearing into the hot, black equatorial night.

Chapter 3

"What do you *mean* Gillian's life is in jeopardy?" Cass said, rushing after Sam.

Sam didn't answer. He tossed his video equipment into the back of the Jeep, his movements fast and astoundingly fluid for his size and bulk. And out of character, because Sam *never* treated the equipment like that. Urgency bit into Cass, along with the whispering excitement she got whenever she sensed something really big going down.

Sam yanked open the driver's-side door, but Cass clamped her hand on his arm. "Speak to me, Sam, or I'm not coming with you."

It was a bluff. He knew it, too—Cass never shied away from potentially breaking news. But for the first time he was angry with her for the very lust that had driven them both to cover one breaking piece after another for the past thirteen months.

"You're just thinking of the story now," he snapped. "I can't

give you any details, not yet. You must first help me get Gillian
out of the country."

"Why?"

"It must remain a secret."

"Come on, Sam, this is *me,* Cass. This is *you,* my camera
guy. Nothing's changed—of course we're after the story. We're
a team, right?"

"This is about Gillian, boss!"

"Okay, okay, walk me through it. But you have got to tell
me what's going on, or I won't know how help you."

He lifted his head to the sky for a moment, gathering himself,
and that's when Cass's suspicion was confirmed—Sam Sekibo
was in love with Gillian Tsabatu. When he lowered his head,
gave her his eyes, they gleamed with emotion. "Boss, if I tell
you, you must swear on your life that you will not use this
story. Nor can you tell a single soul what I am about to reveal
to you—not until Gillian is safely out of the country."

"Sam—"

His eyes narrowed. "Make me that promise."

As he spoke, Cass caught sight of Jack marching down the
driveway towards them with all the purpose of a Mack truck.
Anxiety rippled through her body. "Look, Sam—" she spoke
fast "—this is my job. It's what I do. It's why I am here." *It's
all that keeps me going.*

She flicked another glance at Jack in the distance. He was
going to try and stop her leaving, she could see it in his posture,
his stride.

"I'd never do anything that would jeopardize Gillian's safety,
Sam. Or yours."

"You jeopardize your own safety all the time, boss."

"Trust me, Samuel."

Trust me.

She'd used those words before to get a story, and not honored
them. She'd done it to get one of the biggest scoops of her life
while working in the Middle East. And now she felt a little ill,
conflict twisting inside.

He hesitated, sucking in breath, chest expanding. "You'll

help get her into the compound? You'll help get her on that chopper?"

Cass glanced at the small crowd gathering on the other side of the gate—Kigalis seeking asylum as violence spread. She did not have the sway to get Gillian into the enclosure, or onto that Black Hawk, any more than those folk had hope of getting into the United States. "I promise I'll try my level best, Sam."

He held her eyes for several long beats. Out of the corner of her eyes Cass saw Jack approaching and her chest tightened with urgency.

"King Savungi and the entire Kigali royal family have been slain," Sam said, quietly. "It happened an hour ago."

"*What?* Are you *sure?* Can you verify this?"

"It's not for a story," he warned. "You promised."

"Yes, yes, of course." Christ, this was big.

"The sole survivor of the massacre is King Savungi's youngest son. He was at a relative's home during the attack. The boy's mother was the king's youngest wife, Gillian's cousin. She phoned Gillian to go save her son just as Zuma's men broke into the palace, mere seconds before she was killed."

"General Charles *Zuma* did this? The king's own cousin?"

He nodded, speaking fast. "Zuma's mother is of the Hinti tribe. Zuma apparently used this to rally the majority Hinti in his bid to seize control of the country, and he's got the new Liberian government on his side. When it gets out that Hinti killed the Vendi king, this will escalate into ethnic slaughter like you've never seen," he whispered urgently. "It will be just a matter of time before they learn the boy is still alive, and that Gillian is harboring the new king of Kigali. We have to get them out before that happens."

"Oh jeez," she whispered, dragging her hand over her hair, damp, thick with the fine dust that had blown up with the chopper. "The Deputy Chief of Mission needs to be apprised of this, Sam."

"No!" Sam gabbed her arm, hard. "You promised, boss."

Jack was nearly on them. Cass heard another chopper coming in for landing.

Conflict churned inside her. Sam was asking her to help smuggle the new king of Kigali into U.S. protection, to change a political outcome. He was asking her to break a journalistic tenet—that of observing and reporting news, not making it.

But she couldn't turn away from Sam, or Gillian. Or a little boy whose entire family had just been massacred. Maybe she could find a way to both keep her promise to Sam— save Gillian—and exploit the story later. Do an inside color narrative, a feature on their escape…on the run with a small king. Excitement braided into her conflict.

"Cass!" Jack's voice boomed over the increasing roar of the incoming chopper and the rustling, churning palm fronds.

Cass closed her eyes. "All right, Sam," she said. "Quickly, tell me how you want to handle this."

"We take the news Jeep, and you help me bring Gillian and the boy back here, into the compound—"

"They won't let them in, Sam! Not if I don't tell Swift who the boy is. Even then, the United States will not interfere with—"

"You can make up something, boss."

"Look, just quit with the boss thing and call me Cass!" Irritable, she swiped sweat from her brow. "Okay, we'll go get them. Get in the Jeep quick, before that soldier tries to stop us. And believe me, Sam, he *will* try."

"Cass. Wait!" Jack barked over noise of the now slowing rotors.

The sound of his voice jolted down her spine. Oh, crap. She couldn't seem to think straight for a moment, a sudden, irrational panic mounting in her that had zero to do with the Zuma-king situation and everything to do with facing Jack, and their past. She couldn't bear another fight. "Come on, Sam, get in!" She moved around the vehicle. Yanking open the passenger door, she climbed in. "Drive, Sam. Go."

Sam fired the ignition, but before he got the Jeep into gear,

Jack's hand slapped down on the hood. "Where in hell do you think are you going?"

Her heart thudded. "Nice to see you too, Jack," she said with a saccharine smile. "So what brings *you* to Kigali?"

He moved around the front of the Jeep, hands fisting over her door. His face tight, eyes sparking daggers. "I don't have time for games, Cass. My team is spearheading the U.S. evacuation, and I need you to stay in the compound."

His voice was low, gravelly. He bent close as he spoke and Cass's heart beat faster. She began to shake inside, suddenly insanely desperate to feel his arms around her. Her eyes grew hot, prickling with hurt.

"You show up on the day of our wedding anniversary, and this is the hello I get?" she whispered, the surge of her emotions catching her by the throat.

Something ripped through his face, then was gone. But his tone softened slightly. "Cass, I've got a job to do, and you need to—"

"It's none of your business where I'm going, Jack. I've got a job to do, too—something you never quite managed to acknowledge. Now please step aside before Samuel runs you over. Drive, Sam," she said through her teeth, glaring straight ahead, past him. "Go to the gate."

Jack reached for his sidearm, his eyes threatening Sam as Sam revved the engine.

"Don't do this, Cass," Jack barked, losing his patience, urgency mounting him. "I am *ordering* you to remain on this compound, understand. You will be evacuated with the—"

"You have absolutely zero authority to order me anywhere, Bannister," she said very coolly between her teeth. "Nor do you have a right to threaten my cameraman. I know the drill—there is explicit protocol to be followed in embassy evacuations. I'm not a State Department employee, nor am I family of one. Swift is the one in charge here, not you. She calls the shots, not you. And if any one your men dares try to stop us leaving through that compound gate, you're going to hear about it from much higher up, understand?"

Jack glowered at her, literally vibrating. "You're going to kill yourself chasing your the next big story, you know that, Cass."

"Then that's my choice. Because I sure as hell don't have anything else to live for."

Her body language, the emotion glittering in her eyes, belied her words. Cass was fighting herself—Jack could see it. Compassion sliced through his chest. "Cass, let me help you—"

"*Help* me? What—you want to save me from myself? Get off your high horse, Jack. I don't need a white knight—what I needed was a husband who could compromise, work as a team."

Desperation surged through Jack. He wanted to grab her, hold her, claw back the lost years, the terrible mistakes, and for a moment he seriously considered knocking her out cold and hauling her like a sack of potatoes over his shoulder and onto the next chopper, for her own damn safety.

"You know what you're doing, Cass, you're running. You won't face me, because you can't face what happened to—"

"Shut up and go to hell!" She spun round in her seat, turning her back on him. "Drive, Sam! Go. Now."

"Don't think of coming back, Cass. We're going to clear out of here within hours."

Revving the jeep engine, Sam wheeled around, tires spinning as they headed down the driveway.

"You need a goddamn intervention, you know that, Rousseau!" he yelled after her. "You're your own worst enemy. You're—"

Jack swore, kicked at the gravel as the jeep spun toward the compound gate, kicking up stones in its wake.

She was right—he had no legal tool to force her. It was insane even to begin to think he could control Cass. Let her chase her next damn story. Let her go down in a smoking ball of wretched glory if she wanted to.

He had a job to do.

He spun around and stalked back up the drive to Swift's

residence. But Jack could not tamp down a spark of fear, a cold sense of foreboding.

She had no idea what she was in for out there.

Chapter 4

Sam hurtled the Jeep through scenes of carnage—no streetlights, no power anywhere, darkness aglow with burning houses. Vehicles lay wrecked, charred along the side of the road, people running, screaming. A tank trundled along the highway topped with drunk soldiers. Women screamed from places Cass couldn't see.

In all her years of foreign correspondence, she'd never experienced anything quite like this—the smell of burned bodies, the diesel. The sound of heavy rap music. Dancing silhouettes in front of flames, and laughter amongst the screams.

Cass's stomach backflipped at the sight of a small pile of bodies at the side of the road. Inside she warred with a human need to help versus a fierce journalistic instinct to cover this story, to let the world know the horror of what was happening here. She glanced at Sam, his profile grim.

"Welcome to hell," Sam said, reading her thoughts. Then he swore. "Up ahead, roadblock!"

Oil drums with fires roaring inside lined the road. Drunk soldiers and rebels fired randomly into the air. Sam floored the gas, wheeling suddenly off-road and bashing through grass and brush before bounding onto a dirt track. "We go around back of her village."

Outside Gillian's simple, square concrete house, a thin dog scuttled across the dirt road. Everything was dark, silent.

Too silent.

Cass and Sam glanced at each other.

"Gillian?" Sam called hesitantly as he edged open the unlocked door.

A groan came from the blackness inside, but the distinct coppery smell was enough to tell Cass something was very wrong. Sam flicked his lighter, found a kerosene lamp. A gold low flickered into the room, making shadows come to life. And Cass gasped.

Gillian lay on the sofa, a bunched-up towel clutched tightly to her stomach. It was saturated with blood. Gillian's hands glistened with it.

"Gut shot," Gillian whispered.

Sam thrust the lantern into Cass's hands and lunged forward, dropping to his knees in front of the sofa. "What happened? How badly are you injured?" He edged the towel off her wound, trying to see.

"I…ran a blockade on the way here, and they shot at me. Hit several times…go, please get the boy. He's in the cellar."

"Go, Cass," Sam said firmly as he reached for a glass of water and put it to Gillian's lips. It was the first time he hadn't called her boss. Cass hesitated, worried about her friend.

"Please," moaned Gillian. "Please, just take the boy, leave me, or…this will be for nothing. His…his name is Christmas Savungi." She struggled to breathe in and Cass heard the gurgle in her friend's chest. Blood dribbled from the corner her mouth. "He's…just five years old. He…has…no one…"

Cass found a candle, lit it, hands shaking with adrenaline.

Creaking open the cellar door, she smelled the scent of hot raw earth. She held the candle up in front of her. And in the darkness she saw a pair of dark, shining eyes. Something grabbed Cass by the throat.

"Christmas?" she whispered, reaching gently for his hand. She felt it slip into hers, small, cool. Emotion ripped through her chest—he felt just like Jacob. And for a strange second she felt as if her son was here, now, in this dark cellar, reaching out to her. And suddenly nothing mattered more to Cass than saving this small, vulnerable child.

She turned around to tell Sam to help Gillian into the Jeep. But as Sam's eyes met hers, she knew.

Gillian hadn't made it.

"Take the boy to the Jeep!" Sam barked, eyes bloodshot. He gently covered Gillian's face with his large hand, closing her eyelids. Moisture sheened down his ebony face, glistening on his high, proud cheekbones as he bent down and breathed a kiss over her lips. He covered her with a sheet.

"We will do this," he snapped, rage crackling from him even in his gentleness. "For her, we do this! Now take the child. And swear on your life you will not tell anyone who he is."

Cass looked at her shrouded friend lying on the sofa—a haunting image in the flickering kerosene glow and lunging shadows. Then she felt Christmas's little hand in hers. She glanced down into those huge, frightened eyes. "I promise," she whispered. "I promise I'll get you out of here, Christmas, okay?"

Sam repeated her words to the child in Kigali. "Be proud, be brave. And tell no one your surname, Christmas. You will be safe that way."

He bit his lip, nodded, a tear tracking down from each eye. And Cass's heart ached.

With Christmas hidden under a coarse gray blanket in the back, Sam barreled the Jeep through burning streets while Cass prayed there would still be choppers at the compound, that Jack would still be there.

If there was one thing Jack was, it was stubborn to a fault, and doggedly reliable when he set himself to a mission. He could save this boy. Cass knew he could, if only she'd be able to convince him.

"How will you get Christmas into America?" Sam yelled as he swerved through smoke-filled darkness.

"I don't know. But I will." *I swear it.*

And Cass realized she'd just crossed a line. No longer was she reporting on this Kigali story, she was making it. And she didn't care. Because she was making a difference, for a child.

"Just hurry! I don't know if they'll still be there."

But as they rounded a bend they hit another blockade. Petrol smoke roiled from burning drums in front of a tank and group of soldiers. "Too late to turn back! Hold on!" Sam jammed on brakes and swerved, trying to run the barricade up the side. Machine-gun fire peppered the vehicle. Sam gasped as bullets thudded into his neck and shoulder, jerking his head sideways. Blood began to spurt from his neck as he slumped onto the steering wheel, horn blaring as they barreled straight toward the firing soldiers.

Monday, December 23, 0359 Zulu

Jack checked his watch, sweat dripping. It was getting even hotter as the hours inched towards dawn. The evacuation was also going faster than initially anticipated, since they'd managed to secure two additional heavy-duty birds from the Ivory Coast military. He watched the lights of another helo materializing from out of a black sky thick with smoke.

Susan Swift stood beside Jack on the patio under the lapa as they waited for the chopper to land. Her children and husband had already been flown to the staging area.

"Are you're sure you're ready to leave, Madame Swift?"

She inhaled deeply, nodded. "Diplomacy has become untenable. I don't even know who to communicate with. We have no means of knowing who is behind this yet."

Jack jerked his chin to the sky. "Here's your ride."

"Thank you."

He stepped away as a message came in through his earpiece. It was the pilot, telling him the Liberian air force had started making low flyovers. It looked as though the civil war could conflagrate into all-out invasion. "Orders are to get everyone out on this last flight," said the pilot.

Jack's chest tightened. He glanced down the drive where Cass had disappeared hours ago. "Negative," he said into his radio. "I need to do one more sweep."

There was a moment of static, or hesitation on the pilot's part. "Officer, that was an order."

"Repeat…you're breaking up…" Jack killed the transmission, spun round to address Swift. "The CBN journalist who was interviewing you earlier—do you know if she has a sat phone? Do you have a contact number?"

"Well, yes, we do. My aide has her number in my office."

"I need it. She's still out there," Jack said.

Swift studied him for a long moment. "As is her right, Officer. She's been in bad situations before. She's a professional—this is her game."

Jack read a whole lot more behind Swift's tone. Here was a strong woman defending another woman's right to a dangerous career.

He flattened his mouth.

Yeah. So it was her right to go get herself killed. Cass had always accused him of trying to stomp on her career. If she wanted to die chasing her next big story, all the power to her. There was no way on earth he could control Cass. They were like oil and water. As much as he still loved his estranged wife, they could never live together.

Second chances were a stupid pipe dream. He'd been kidding himself too long.

He sucked it up, and keyed his radio. "We're good to go, clearing out…"

Chapter 5

Cass lurched across the seat, shouldering Sam sideways as she grabbed the wheel. Blood flowed hot over her bare arm. She elbowed his knee, dislodging his foot from the gas pedal, and the Jeep decelerated slightly. Cass used the moment to ram the stick shift into second gear, grinding against the clutch as the vehicle bounded down into a ditch. She swung the wheel to the right, slowing the Jeep's progress, crashing through brush. Cass swore, but blindly kept going.

Finally she managed to slow enough in dense undergrowth to reach down for the brake. The Jeep stopped, hidden by trees.

Heart pounding, sweat dripping, Cass listened. She heard gunfire, but the soldiers must have been so inebriated or high that they hadn't got it together to come after them.

Quickly, Cass felt for Sam's pulse. Nothing.

Christmas?

She swung around, peeled off the blanket. The boy peered

up at her, dead silent, wide-eyed. Shaking. *Oh, God*. A child should never have to experience this kind of terror. Tears filled her eyes. "It's going to be fine, I promise, with all my heart. I'm going to do this."

But how?

With a trembling hand Cass wiped blood and dirt off her mouth. Then she sweated to maneuver Sam's massive frame out from the driver's seat, stilling every few seconds to listen to the jungle, to the sounds of gunfire, to see if the men were coming.

She finally managed to pull him into the passenger seat, and she climbed into the bloodied driver's seat. Fighting exhaustion, Cass realized suddenly that she had no idea how to get back to the compound, other than along that blockaded road.

She had her sat phone in her backpack. But who was she going call—911? She laughed harshly out loud. Needing to hear the sound of her own voice, to validate herself.

Yeah right. *You wanted this—you wanted to push the limits.*

But she did not want a kid in it all. Not a little boy, vulnerable, dependent on her. A boy the same age as Jacob had been.

As she leaned forward and turned the key in the ignition, she heard truck engines approaching. Adrenaline kicked—the only place she could think to hide until it was light was Gillian's house. Cass headed down a side road and reconnected with the main road several miles further east. Retracing her route she drove slowly, watchful of the flickering fires, praying it was still quiet in Gillian's village.

She'd hide with Christmas in the cellar until daybreak.

And then she'd have to figure out what to do next. Because no way was she going to get help from the embassy now.

They'd all be gone by dawn. Jack, too. Probably damning her to die for her story. She deserved it.

She was on her own. Always had been, even when they were together.

But this innocent boy called Christmas did not deserve this.

She had to get him out of this dark and burning nightmare. Come hell or high water.

And she had to do it alone.

Monday, December 23, 0612

Cass creaked open the cellar door and peered out into the small living room. A hazy orange dawn filtered through the drawn curtains. It was hot, muggy, the scent of the death pungent. She crept out, her stomach clenching as she bypassed Gillian's shrouded form on the sofa.

Carefully, Cass lifted the edge of the curtain with the backs of her fingers. Her muscles went rigid—there was a group of men down the road, looting a house. It wouldn't be long before they reached this one.

Hurriedly she moved to the kitchen. In the fridge she found fruit, bottles of water. She took these to Christmas in the cellar. Then she grabbed her backpack and stuffed what other food she could find into it. Hastily she cobbled together a first aid kit from the bathroom cabinet, and exchanged her blouse and skirt for a pair of pants and a T-shirt from Gillian's closet. She rinsed Sam's blood from her face and arms.

But before she was done, she heard the men yelling outside. She bolted back down into the cellar, leaving her pack and sat phone on the kitchen table.

She held Christmas tight, praying they'd leave, that if they entered the house, the shrouded body might spook them off.

Then she heard the Jeep's engine starting outside to the sound of cheers and random gunshots.

She cursed, tears of frustration burning into her eyes as she heard them driving it away. She wondered what they'd done with Sam's body—she'd left him in the passenger seat.

Now she didn't even have transport.

Despair, fatigue, heat crowded out logic for a moment.

How on earth was she going to get this little boy out of this country in crisis? She didn't speak the language, she stuck out like a sore thumb, didn't know the way…she'd relied on Sam for so much.

Her thoughts were broken by a sound somewhere in the house. Cass tensed, listening, her heart jackhammering.

She heard it again.

Her sat phone! In her bag upstairs.

With shaking hands she crawled out. Hunkering down on the floor behind the table so no one would glimpse her through the kitchen window, she reached for the phone.

"Hello?" she said quietly. Nervous.

"Cass. It's Jack. Where are you?"

Emotion surged through her, lodging hard in her throat. Nothing, not one thing in this entire world was more welcome than hearing his voice, and for a moment she was unable to speak.

"Cass, are you all right?" The deep, measured calm of his voice steeled her. Cass cleared her throat, not wanting to come across as weak or uncertain to him. Or afraid. "I…I'm fine." But her voice clearly belied her words.

"Cass, speak to me—what's going on?"

"Jack. I'm in deep trouble."

Jack watched the rotors of the chopper speeding up as he spoke, the pilot making a motion for him to come. The DCM was finally on board. She had received another call from Washington, which had delayed their departure for over an hour. Jack had tried to delayed it further. At war within himself, he'd capitulated and called Cass, trying her phone several times, growing increasingly worried when there was no answer.

Now his stomach knotted at the sound of her voice. And he knew Cass would not ask for his help unless something was very seriously amiss. He closed his eyes for a moment, torn, seconds ticking away, the sound of the rotors increasing.

"My cameraman is dead, Jack. I've been hiding at a colleague's house, in the cellar. She's been shot dead, too and her village is being looted. The roads are blocked. Our vehicle is gone."

The rotors roared to full speed, downdraft whipping palm fronds into a frenzy. This was it, last chopper out. The rebels had breached the army blockade on the highway. It was just a matter of hours, maybe even minutes, before they reached the compound.

"Cass—" he said.

"I need you, Jack."

His heart swelled, his fist tightening on the phone. This was what he wanted—wasn't it? For her to need him, for one last chance to get it right, to atone for his own role in messing up their marriage?

He glanced at chopper.

Once that bird left…

Chapter 6

Jack swore.

He argued with himself he would be quick. He'd try and call for an evac once he returned with her to the compound. But at least he'd be trying—he'd never live with himself if he didn't.

"Hold on, Cass," he said into the sat phone as he made a flicking motion with his hand, telling the pilot to take off. He keyed his radio. "U.S. civilian is stranded behind enemy lines," he barked. "I'm going in to assist."

He killed the transmission before the pilot could respond, or remind him that the compound itself could come under siege within hours. He switched back to the sat phone. "Where's your friend's house?" He strode swiftly toward one of the military jeeps on site as he spoke. Jack told himself he was not abandoning the chargés d'affaires, his mission, his country, by going to look for Cass in hostile territory. He was doing his duty.

As a husband.

And it was about bloody time. He'd lost enough to know how much he wanted now, and what deep compromises he was prepared to make for a second chance.

"I'm not sure, Jack. It was dark. We headed out on the eastbound route, but then Sam took several back road detours to avoid blockades. He…he was shot in the neck…when we tried to run one of the roadblocks."

Jack fired the jeep's ignition. "Does your phone have GPS?" He barreled out of the compound gates as he spoke. They were now unguarded, the crowds of asylum-seekers milling about, restless, some angry at the Americans for pulling out and leaving them to uncertain fate in their own country. One threw a rock at Jack's vehicle as he passed.

"It does—" She gave him the coordinates. Jack punched them into the military vehicle's GPS mapping system. Then he laid on the gas, racing eastward. The sound of artillery shelling rattled to the west.

"Why did you leave the compound, Cass?" he said, fists tight on the wheel. He wanted to keep her talking. And he needed to know.

"I…my friend needed help."

He was silent for a second. "It wasn't for a story?"

There was another beat of silence, a shift in her tone. "No," she said quietly.

He sucked in air, fists tightening even further on wheel. "Don't move from where you are, understand? Keep your phone on, and make sure it has a clear line with no obstruction to the sky. It's not going to work if you take it down into the cellar. It's probably why I couldn't get through earlier."

"You tried earlier?"

"Yes."

"Jack?"

He inhaled. "I'm still here."

"Thank you," she whispered.

Ambushed by a fierce surge of emotion, he signed off.

Above, in the western sky, the Black Hawk carrying Swift grew smaller, metal glimmering in the first violent rays of the morning sun.

Daylight revealed a post-apocalyptic nightmare. Black smoke snaked from burning villages and vultures circled above dull green trees. Scavenger dogs and baboons scampered between bodies, and the gutted wrecks of burned-out vehicles were strewn along the road. But the sound of shelling had ceased and an eerie lull pressed down with the heat of the new day—perhaps a hangover from the night of violence. Jack wondered how long the lull might last before the next wave.

Sweat slid down his brow as he saw blackened oil drums and a coil of razor wire across the road ahead, soldiers with red bandannas and armbands passed out against trucks. This must be the barricade that Cass and her cameraman had run into earlier. He swallowed at the thought of how close he'd come to losing her, to never getting a chance to make things right.

Quietly, Jack swung the wheel, ducking off the tarred road. He followed a rutted dirt track into dense trees. If he played it calm, using the GPS mapping software in his military vehicle, he could keep moving toward Cass via a series of off-road routes through the old rubber and cacao plantations that covered the foothills in this area.

The flashing GPS dots grew closer and closer. He was almost there.

He neared a small cluster of houses with tin roofs. The stench of carrion was powerful here. He saw more bodies, an abandoned tricycle. A kid's bloodied shoe. His mouth turned bitter.

So this is Christmas…and look what you've done…

Inhaling deeply, he pulled up outside the plain square house registering on the GPS.

The cameraman's large body lay crumpled on the packed red dirt outside, like tossed-aside garbage, tire tracks at his side. Rage mushroomed in Jack. His gaze flicked left and right as he reached for his assault weapon and clicked off the safety.

Gun leading, he crept round the side of house, peered in the window. Through a small gap in the drapes he saw a body on the sofa, covered in a sheet drenched with blood. His mouth turned dry.

Once he'd circled the perimeter, Jack tried the front door. It was locked. He kicked it open. Weapon leading, he entered the home. A wall of humidity slammed into him, thick with the overpowering stench of death. He scanned the small living room, saw Cass's pack and sat phone on the kitchen table.

Cellar, she said cellar.

He spun around, saw the cellar door, but before he could move toward it, the door creaked slowly ajar. Jack raised his weapon, pulse quickening. The door opened farther and Cass emerged, her eyes dazed from the darkness underground.

Raw emotion slammed so hard and fast through Jack he didn't think about what he did next. Grabbing her by the shoulders, he pulled her tight against his body, and he just held. And for a nanosecond time stood still, the years between them slipping away. Just as quickly, Jack felt awkward, and pulled away.

But he saw that her eyes shimmered with tears.

Swallowing, he turned away, disguising his own overwhelming feelings with action. "Come," he said grabbing her pack and sat phone from the table. "We don't have one second to spare, not if we're going to make it back to the compound and get a flight out of this hellhole before—"

"Jack, wait."

Something in the firmness of her tone stopped him, and he looked into her eyes.

Her gaze flicked nervously to the cellar door. A sense of uneasiness curled into him. "Cass—" He stepped up to her. "Why *did* you come here? What happened to your colleague, exactly?"

She ran her tongue over her teeth—he knew the gesture well. She was cooking up some story. Irritation flared. "Look here, Cass, Liberian jets have started making low flyovers—civil war could erupt into a full Liberian invasion at any moment.

For all we know the new Liberian government initiated this instability. No one understands what is going down yet, or who is behind what faction. It's—"

"Jack," she said quietly. "There's a small boy in the cellar. We have to take him with us."

He stared at her, precious seconds leaking by. "A U.S. citizen?"

Her lids flickered. And he knew, he just knew her too well—she was going to lie to him.

Irritation segued into a burst of frustration—he and Cass had such a way of bringing out the worst in each other, butting heads all the way. He was kidding himself, it would never work between them. "We're running out time. And my orders are clear—only U.S. citizens. If he's local, we leave him!"

More precious seconds slid by as Cass battled with her next choice. She knew how stubborn Jack could be and how much a true soldier he was. If he had orders to leave behind Kigali locals, he would. His crack infiltration team would not have survived their missions without clear and sometimes harsh guidelines. If she told him the Kigali royal family had been slaughtered, and that the little five-year-old orphan hiding in the cellar was now technically king of a country in chaos, Jack would be compelled to inform the DCM immediately.

She didn't want to put him in that position. She did not want to cost him his career.

But she'd made a promise to Sam and a vow to the boy.

She could not allow Sam and Gillian to have sacrificed their lives in vain.

Cass steeled herself, meeting Jack's eyes directly, a little quiver shooting through her chest at the intensity in his gaze, and what it did her body. "The boy is the son of an African-American employee of the U.S. embassy," she said. "The child was visiting Kigali friends and got separated from his family during the attack."

Jack's eyes narrowed, his blue stare crackling. The temperature under the tin roof increased as the sun grew more fierce outside, and humidity inside grew thicker. Perspiration gleamed on Jack's skin.

"Don't do this, Cass," he growled, low, angry. "Do not lie to me! I've seen the manifest. I know who worked at the embassy and no one said a child was missing. Tell me who the child is!" he demanded.

Cass swallowed, her cheeks going hot, sweat pearling between her breasts. The image of Christmas, his big, frightened eyes, the feeling of his little hand in hers, washed through her.

"It shouldn't matter whose child it is," she said very quietly, sensing the time running away, the last window of hope closing. Panic tightened her chest. "He's just a five-year-old orphan, Jack. He's got no one—" Her voice caught on a sudden lump of emotion. She took Jack's large hands in her own. "Please… this is a child we *can* still save."

Jack stared at Cass, memories, pain, suddenly thick, visceral, lacing into the damp, hot air. More precious seconds ticked by, and he allowed them to slip, unable to do otherwise as he looked into his estranged wife's eyes, the window into her torment no matter how much she tried to hide—or run—from it.

Because suddenly Jack understood what was going on with Cass.

She was thinking of Jacob.

And now so was he.

"Jack," she urged softly. "I know I've crossed a line. But now that I'm here, now that you're here…we *have* to take this boy with us. We cannot leave him."

Jack raked his hand through his dust-thickened hair, his body damp with sweat as the equatorial heat pressed down. "Cass, I have orders. They do *not* include evacuating locals."

"Fine." Her mouth flattened and her eyes turned cold. "Then give me one of your guns, and a knife, anything you can spare. I'll do this on my own."

"You'll die."

"At least I'll die trying! At least I won't have to live the rest of my life trying to hide from the memory of…" Shock registered on her face as she realized what she was saying. The rest of her words stuck in her throat and hung, unspoken, quivering between them. Tears pooled in her eyes.

"Oh, Cass—" Jack whispered, reaching up and cupping the side of her jaw. She leaned into him slightly, needing him, the human connection in this living nightmare. Jack's heart swelled with compassion. "Cass, I know what this child symbolizes to you, but—"

Before he could finish, a silent, frightened boy stepped out from behind the cellar door, his luminous dark eyes focused intently, solely, on Jack.

Jack froze.

The boy was the same size and age as his son had been when he died, and for an insane, head-over-heels, crazy about-face moment, Jack saw Jacob standing there.

He cursed, lifting his face to the ceiling, as if the sheer force of gravity might hold back the brutal surge of emotion churning inside him. How could this be? It was like some freaking sign—seeing Cass on their wedding anniversary, being confronted by a five-year-old boy that he *could* still save, together. With Cass.

Like they hadn't been together for their son. At Christmastime. When they'd lost him.

Cass touched his arm. A powerful current of connection jolted through him. And he just knew why he must help her.

It was for Jacob.

For his memory.

It was a way to give some meaning to their son's death.

It was the way to a second chance.

Chapter 7

Jack crouched down, balancing on the balls of his feet as placed his hands on the boy's small shoulders. "Don't worry, big guy," he said gently in Kigali. "We're going to look after you. My name's Jack. Can you tell me your name, son?"

Tears pooled in the boy's eyes. "Christmas," he whispered.

Jack shot a glance at Cass. "You have got to be kidding me."

She shook her head.

"What about his last name?"

"Gillian didn't say."

Jack regarded her intently. "Are you *sure?*"

"Of course I'm sure."

Jack's gaze pierced hers, looking for a lie, something that might tell him Cass knew more. But right now, all he could see was raw emotion and he was imbued with an eerie sense of something bigger, something surreal going on here.

"Will you help us, Jack?"

He looked away. And Cass knew he was struggling. He had to be thinking of Jacob, of what they'd lost. Her gaze fell to his large, capable hands resting on the boy's shoulders, and she caught sight of the gold band against his tanned skin. Shock jolted through Cass.

Jack still wore his wedding ring.

She opened her mouth, but was at a loss for words, a maelstrom of feelings riding through her, and automatically her thumb sought her own naked ring finger. Her throat choked with tears.

"Yes," Jack said, turning back to face her. "We'll take him."

Emotion hiccupped hard and sore through her chest and in that moment Cass loved Jack with all her heart, the way she always had. The way she'd forgotten how. Because she knew what sacrifice he had just agreed to make, how it could cost him his career with the military, which defined him. And he was doing it for her.

For the memories they shared.

For what they had lost.

For Jacob.

She crouched down to Christmas's eye level, reached out, touched Jack's arm. "Thank you, Jack," she whispered.

His mouth tightened, a small muscle pulsing at his jaw. And Cass felt a tenuous rope of compassion, grief, quivering between them, bonding them. They were in this together.

Monday, December 23, 0700 Zulu

Cass sat beside Jack in the army jeep, Christmas in her lap. His little hands gripped her shirt and she cupped his head against her breast in an effort to keep him from seeing what was happening in the streets and fields and plantations of his country.

Jack's features were resolute, his hands tense on the wheel. He spun off the track suddenly, heading between the trees of an old rubber plantation. "There's another roadblock ahead—could see by the smoke. We can take a back route through the plantations in the foothills, but it will take a lot longer."

"How do you know so much about this place, Jack? How long have you been here?"

"Six months. My team was helping the new Kigali army develop a training plan."

Surprise washed through Cass. "*You* were part of that group? Swift told me there was a twelve-man team here training local troops."

"Yep. That was us."

Cass studied his rugged profile, a new curiosity rustling into a whole mess of conflicting emotions. Her gaze went once again to the wedding ring on his sun-browned hand, and she felt hurt, guilt. That ring had once represented so much hope and promise.

"More smoke above the canopy there," Jack said with a jerk of his chin. "The violence is still spreading. Hell knows who is behind this thing."

Guilt deepened. Cass looked away, cupping Christmas's head tighter against her body. The poor child was so exhausted he'd fallen asleep in the midst of this chaos. Sorrow and empathy swelled inside her as she held the boy—it was such a human, maternal feeling to protect a small and innocent child. How her arms had ached to hold Jacob again in this way, how her very soul had felt like an empty hole when he died.

Jack swore a streak suddenly and spun the wheel of the jeep. He steered into dense undergrowth. A monkey screeched and a large bird startled out from the foliage with a cry.

"Rebels?" Cass whispered as they came to a stop. It was dark and hot like a sauna under the trees. Jack sat for a moment, silent, scrolling through his GPS mapping system. "Yeah—we're cut off. No other way back." He checked his watch, muscles rolling smoothly under his sun-browned skin. His dark hair was damp.

"Even if we do find a route, chances are they've taken the

compound already." He reached for the radio, keyed it, calling his detachment commander.

"I'm trapped behind enemy lines with a U.S. civilian, Captain. She's a CBN reporter." Jack shot Cass a glance as he spoke, his attention flicking briefly to Christmas huddled and still sleeping in her arms. But he said nothing about the boy. Nor about the fact the reporter was his estranged wife. "We're going to try head north, up into the mountains. We'll cross into Ivory Coast from there. I'll maintain radio contact."

He signed off.

"You want to go over those mountains?" she asked, incredulous. "That jungle is impenetrable, Jack, no tracks, nothing. No one goes there, and if they do, they don't always come out alive."

He exhaled heavily, pulling a waterproof pouch with contour map out of his pocket. He studied it a while in silence, then restarted the ignition without looking at her. "There'll be less chance of violence in that region," he said bluntly.

She'd pushed him out of his comfort zone and he was annoyed by it.

"Are you sure it's the best—"

"It's the only way," he snapped. "We try and go back into that mess and we're not going to stand a chance. I'm not going to put you and the boy into that kind of a hostile situation. You want my help, you play by my rules."

His brusque tone instantly got under her skin.

"Your rules? That's what it's always been about, Jack, hasn't it? Your rules. Your game. Never any compromise, no teamwork in—"

His eyes flared to hers, crackling, angry. "Do you want my help or not? Because I sure as hell can leave you here anytime you want."

She opened her mouth, ready with a biting retort, but thought better of it, swiping the dirt-layered sweat from her brow instead. Cass hadn't realized just how much she'd allowed stress, fatigue, fear to get better of her, and she'd slipped into knee-jerk habit of bickering with Jack. That had been a mistake.

Because he was making huge sacrifice—he was helping her smuggle a non-U.S. citizen over the border against his orders. And he was doing it because of what they'd shared in the past.

There'd be hell to pay if he found out she'd known all along that Christmas was the new king, that she knew who was behind the coup and had not told him. But if Cass gave him that knowledge now, it would force Jack into an even worse situation. She couldn't do that to him.

In silence they bumped and maneuvered up into the hills. The going was tedious on a track of red dirt riddled with giant potholes, some big enough to swallow an army jeep whole, or at least break the axle.

The jungle grew thicker, creeping, crawling in from both sides, reclaiming the narrow trail, covering the sky above. Small rivers now trickled through the potholes, eroding soil further. The scent grew verdant. Bright birds darted under the canopy and the monkeys became more exotic, some with old men's faces, others with tufts of facial hair or bright behinds. Vines, thick as a man's arm, snaked from monstrous branches.

And as they inched up to higher altitude, a hot mist began to roll down from the dull green peaks, swamping the atmosphere with fine droplets and a whispering sense of unease. Odd cries came from the forest, making Cass edgy. And as they crossed a wide riverbed in a muddy gully, the jeep died.

"Out of gas," Jack said matter-of-factly as he turned around, leaning into the back of the jeep for Cass's pack.

"Jack…I'm sorry."

"We need to go on foot from here, anyway." He began stuffing her pack with his GPS, radio, knife, water purifying tablets, flint, flares and other gear. He got out of the jeep, trekked through the mud, and dumped the gear on a flat rock at the base of a steep, rocky cliff wall.

"No," she called after him, "I mean I'm sorry about what I said earlier, about rules, compromise."

He shot her a glance, but said nothing. Instead he helped Christmas out the vehicle. Crouching down to the boy's eye level, he said in Kigali, "You go sit with that gear and guard it, my little man. Can you do that?"

Christmas nodded, eyes intent on Jack.

Jack turned to Cass. "I need your help to push the jeep down into that gully over there, into the undergrowth. Don't want to leave a blazing beacon in the middle of the riverbed marking our way."

Reaching into the vehicle, he made sure the gears were in Neutral.

"Jack, I mean it. I'm sorry. It was…inappropriate, a force of habit."

"Please just push, Cass." He shouldered his weight into the vehicle, guiding it with the steering wheel, sweat dripping instantly. "C'mon, give it some muscle, will you? The mud's thick here."

But she put her hands on her hips, glowered at him. "You're doing it again, Jack. You're avoiding the issue, the thing that tripped us up every time."

He stood up, swiped sweat from his brow. "Jesus, Cass. I'm trying to get you to safety—"

"And then what?"

He sighed. "Look," he said quietly, "it cut both ways. You wanted me to quit the military, that's what it boiled down to, but this is *me*. This is the guy you married. I am a soldier."

"A soldier who married a foreign news correspondent, Jack. I didn't hide who I was, either. And it wasn't easy for me to give up one job after another, following you from base to base. With each transfer or promotion you got, I had to quit yet another job at some other small-town station. I gave up my international career for you and Jacob, so I could be a good mom, a decent wife. That's not something you'd ever have even begun to think of doing for us."

He rubbed his brow, stepped closer. "Maybe we just tried to tie the knot too early, Cass, before working out the nuts and bolts of how this thing was going to work."

She swallowed at his proximity, the way his muscles bunched and gleamed from exertion, the way his hair hung

damp on his brow. Poignant memories curled, cool, through
the hot mist—the pleasure of making love with him. Jacob's
birth, which he'd missed. Their son's first birthday, for which
Jack had been absent. Their first wedding anniversary—Jack
on yet another tour of duty.

Adrenaline, the hot zones, they fueled them both. It was
the stuff of their energy, the fire behind their passion. They'd
met in a war zone, and fallen in love in one. Thriving on the
danger. But her pregnancy had changed it all.

Cass had been forced to quit the race.

And she'd tried, by God, she'd tried. Jacob had been the
glue that had kept her struggling to make it all work.

But when she lost Jacob, she'd needed her job back. She'd
needed to throw her pain into something. Their home had felt
so empty. *She* had felt so empty. She couldn't just sit there,
alone, being a military wife for an absent husband who held
his duty for his country above his will to make his marriage
work.

And Cass knew she couldn't have asked him to be otherwise,
any more than he could ask her.

That's why it hadn't worked and never would, even as
fiercely as the electricity still crackled between them.

"Yeah, maybe," she said. "Maybe we should never have even
tried." Cass placed the palms of her hands on the back of the
jeep. "Let's get this done with. Let's get over those wretched
mountains. Then we can move on."

The going was tough, the mud slippery, and as the vehicle
jolted forward down the incline, barreling into the gully, Cass
slipped and splatted face-forward into the mud. Pain sparked
from her arm.

"Hey, easy there," Jack said, reaching down to take her
hand. He helped her to her feet, holding her close, the palm of
his hand on her ribs, just under her breast, as he steadied her.
Cass's heart stammered and her cheeks heated. It was the fall,
she told herself, not the proximity of his body, the way he was
touching her. Yet she couldn't get herself to back away.

"Does it hurt anywhere?"

"No," she lied.

"You sure? I know you, Cass—"

"I said I'm fine."

"Good." He wiped the mud from her cheek as he spoke, a tenderness softening his stark blue eyes. Cass was suddenly conscious of the heat, a flock of birds with red beaks flying overhead, the sounds of the jungle, butterflies in the sky. "Thanks," she said softly.

Jack stared at her, his eyes changing to a moody indigo. He started to slide his hand down her arm, slowly, his body leaning forward, his head angling slightly. Cass's vision blurred as his mouth neared hers, and every molecule in her body responded, waiting for his kiss. But suddenly she caught a movement behind him, and stiffened.

"Jack!"

He dropped his hand, stepped back. "Sorry," he said brusquely. "Won't happen again—"

"No," she hissed. "Behind you. Elephants!"

He spun around just as a large herd charged out the trees and down the opposite bank into the riverbed.

"They're charging us!" Cass yelled as she spun around to flee.

Chapter 8

Jack grabbed Cass's arm, halting her. "They're not charging us," he hissed, eyes fixed on the herd. "Elephants can't take inclines like that slowly. But whatever you do, *don't run*—out here, only food runs. Now slowly go up onto those rocks, take Christmas and work your way a little higher. They won't climb those boulders. We can watch them from up there."

"*Watch* them?"

He laughed softly, eyes bright, clearly exhilarated by the sight of the prehistoric gargantuans. "We're sure as hell not going anywhere else as long as they're in our path."

From up on their rock ledge, they watched the elephants coming down to drink and splash red mud over each other. Awe overcame Cass. "They're so quiet," she whispered. "We never even heard them coming."

Jack nodded. "So much for making a noise like an elephant." He put his arm around Christmas and pointed. "See? That one's the matriarch, Christmas. She's the boss, and the family has to listen to her no matter what. It's their best chance of survival."

Cass smiled and cleared her throat theatrically. "Maybe we should take a lesson from that."

He looked at her, grinned, his gorgeous blue eyes twinkling like a summertime lake. Her chest tightened. They'd almost kissed, and it had just happened. And she'd really wanted it to.

She glanced at his hand, the gleam of gold around his finger. Tears welled as easily as the smile that had sneaked up on her. She swiped them angrily away, turning her head so he wouldn't see.

She still loved him. Dammit.

She still wanted him and she couldn't have him, because it could never work.

"Cass?"

She sniffed, wiping her nose, but wouldn't turn to face him.

"What is it, Cass?" He touched her arm, his strength, his power suffusing into her, like it always had.

Still turned away, she said, "Why do you still wear the ring, Jack?"

"Why don't you wear yours anymore?"

"Why should I?" she said quietly.

"Because we're not divorced."

She turned slowly to look at him. "That's only because neither of us wanted to face each other long enough to go through with it."

His mouth flattened. "Speak for yourself, Cass."

They fell quiet as they heard Christmas laugh at the antics of the two baby elephants. A baboon watched them, too, a short distance from the water's edge where a crocodile had disappeared under the surface.

"Do you want to do it—" he said, eyes on the herd "—make a commitment to end it, now, on our anniversary? It's an appropriate enough day to deal with it."

Bitterness laced his words.

"What I want to do is save this boy," she replied, her own words crisp.

"I wear the ring, Cass," he said very quietly, "for the same reason I still carry this." Jack removed the crumpled, tattered photo from his breast pocket, held it out to her.

She turned to look.

And her heart punched.

In Jack's hand was a photograph of Jacob—Cass's arms around him, a huge smile on her face, happiness twinkling in her eyes. She'd carried more weight then, and it was flattering. They were seated in front of a Christmas tree at Cass's parents' home—in the mountain town where they'd married. "Christmas town," Cass had called it, because in winter it always looked just like a perfect Christmas card.

It was the last Christmas they'd ever had together. It was the Christmas before Jacob was killed.

The pain that twisted through Cass's chest was so powerful and so sudden, she couldn't breathe for a moment. Slowly she tore her eyes from the frozen, crumpled memory to meet Jack's gaze. And she noticed for the first time the new stress lines that fanned out from his eyes, the way the creases that bracketed his strong mouth had grown deeper. It was a rugged, handsome face, and she loved it with all her heart.

She began to shake inside, afraid to say anything, to go further down this dangerous path, but could not turn away, either.

"And I wear our ring, Cass, for the same reason I always find a small church somewhere in the world at this time of year, where I remember. And I pray for a way to find reason, to make sense of it all. For a way to make it right."

Guilt twisted through her.

Jack had suffered as much as she had. She looked at Christmas, who was still watching the elephants. And an uncanny feeling of unreality wrapped like the hot mist around her. "It should have been me who died in that plane crash, Jack," she whispered. "Not my son."

"*Our* son, Cass."

Her mouth tightened. She knew what she was doing. She was trying to protect herself by locking him out, holding her grief to her chest, private, personal, all her very own. As if letting it go would somehow betray Jacob's memory.

It was her way of keeping her son alive.

"You should have gotten professional help, Cass, like the docs said. You have some kind of survivor's guilt. That's why you keep running, chasing these stories, isn't it? You're daring the world to kill you—as if it might make it right that it took Jacob instead."

"Damn, you, Jack." She got up, arms tightly folded over her stomach. He was forcing her to an edge, an abyss. Holding on to her pain was the one thing that held her together.

But he was right, and she knew it.

Her doctors had told her to see a shrink after the plane crash in Alaska—she had been in denial then, and perhaps she still was now. She had never moved beyond that first stage of grief towards acceptance. Suddenly she felt Christmas's warm little hand reaching up for hers, tugging to go closer to see the baby elephant being bathed. Emotion pricked into her eyes. Somehow that path up ahead into the jungle and over the border into Ivory Coast seemed more daunting than ever.

And this little boy was urging her to take the next step.

She had to do it, go forward. And she had to allow Jack to guide them. Again Cass wondered what strange fate of magic had brought them all to this juncture at this particular time.

Jack stood up, came to her side, touched her shoulder. "We should move," he said.

"It won't work, Jack," she said quietly. "You know it won't."

"Just keep moving forward, Cass."

December 23, 1800 Zulu

Night fell like a hot velvet curtain and thirst plagued them as they trekked yet higher and higher, Jack hacking a path with a machete, his muscles gleaming in the light of his headlamp. Cass swatted bugs away from her face.

Wildlife and terrain now presented a different kind of danger. The sound of frogs filled the air, a shrill rising and falling chorus. Something rustled through the leaves at Cass's feet. She gasped as Jack spun round and whacked his machete down, severing the head of a brown snake, thick as her leg. Its body continued to writhe. "Gaboon viper. Stay back from the head." He ordered crisply. "A reflex bite could still kill you."

"Oh, dear God," she whispered as she gathered Christmas into her arms.

"We'll stop for the night, up ahead," Jack said, watching her in the light of his headlamp. "Looks like we could all use some rest."

He found them a large bombax with buttress roots big enough to make caves. Clearing the forest debris out of one of the deep pleats in the smooth trunk, he checked it was safe. Jack gave them bug juice, and together they huddled into the small enclosure, protected by the giant roots.

Jack didn't sleep. He listened to the sounds of the jungle, marveling at how it felt to have Cass in his arms, the smooth swell of her breast against his chest, the sensation of her hair against his face. He loved her even more, if it was possible. Christmas curled at her side, snoring softly as he slept. Jack's heart went out to the child. He wondered what the future would hold for the small boy once they crossed the border—an orphan in Africa, sadly, was nothing out of the ordinary.

Just before dawn, Jack tensed at a particular sound, different from the ambient chorus of the jungle. He shook Cass awake gently, put his finger to his lips, whispered in her ear, "Soldiers coming. Don't move—keep Christmas quiet if he wakes."

She jolted upright, eyes wide. "Where are you going?"

"Up into the tree over there, where I can get a good shot, just in case. Best scenario, they don't see us."

Or smell us.

Jack was worried about the distinct scent of bug spray on their skin. A good tracker would pick it up instantly.

He shimmied up the tree, positioned himself in a fork. Within minutes he heard voices, growing louder. Kigali language. Raucous laughter. From the sounds of it, the troop was merry—maybe high on drugs and drink. They'd be lethal in this condition, but maybe not alert enough to notice Cass and the boy, or him up in the tree as they passed beneath. He motioned to Cass again to stay dead quiet. Her eyes were huge. She nodded, hugging Christmas to her chest.

The pale gray light of dawn fingered and dappled down through the canopy just as he caught sight of the first man. Glistening skin. Red bandanna.

Rebels.

Jack's throat tasted bitter as he saw blood on their fatigues. He could smell death and old sweat on them, but he held steady as seven men passed beneath his branch. The man at the rear paused suddenly, and Jack's pulse kicked.

The solider turned, raising stock to shoulder as he scanned the undergrowth—he'd detected something unusual. Slowly Jack lowered his eye to his gun sight, curled his finger against his trigger. He'd taken care not to hack a path into their night hide with his machete, but the men would have seen their earlier tracks.

But just as he was about to squeeze, the men up ahead yelled for their comrade. The man took one last glance around, and moved on.

Relief washed through Jack. He slid down the tree, went to Cass, cupped her face. "They're gone."

"Oh, thank, God, Jack. Thank you. I can't believe we're still alive, that nothing ate us in the night."

Her eyes were luminous, soft like he hadn't seen them in years. And she looked unusually vulnerable. Even all messed up like this, she had never been more beautiful to him. And Jack could not help what came next. He bent down, and brushed her lips softly with his.

Chapter 9

Jack felt her sharp catch of breath, then to his surprise, Cass opened her lips a little more, welcoming his kiss, and inside he melted. His heart wanted to say, *I love you. I always have.*

He wanted to try to do it right this time, now that they were battle-scarred and world-weary—now that he'd learned what was truly important in his life.

He'd give it all up if he could have her again. If she'd let him. And the answer he could feel in her body bolstered and fueled and strengthened his resolve. "I'm going to get you both out of here," he whispered against her lips.

A small tear leaked out from the corner of her eye and he felt her hand seeking his, slipping into his. He felt her fingering his wedding ring.

"I'm afraid," she whispered.

"I'll protect you."

"It's not the jungle I'm afraid of, Jack."

He looked into her eyes. And he knew what she was talking

about. "Trust in me, Cass. We can do this. We—" He was interrupted by a radio transmission, which stirred Christmas awake.

Jack surged to his feet, keyed his radio. "Come in—"

Cass dug into her backpack as Jack stepped slightly away. She removed a military ready-to-eat-meal pouch, and tore off the top. She handed it to Christmas, showing him how to eat it. "And guess what, Christmas," she said with a smile, "it's turkey, and today is Christmas Eve. How cool is that?"

Christmas studied her uncomprehendingly with large, round eyes as he tucked heartily into the meal.

Jack kept an eye on them as he listened to his commander, who was now at the Ivory Coast staging camp from where the Marines were flying personnel out to the *U.S.S. Shackleton.*

"Bannister, we just got news that the entire Kigali royal family was assassinated in the early hours of yesterday morning—all apart from the youngest son. And we've learned that King Savungi's cousin, General Charles Zuma, is behind the coup. Word is also leaking out that a local television news reporter, Gillian Tsabatu, a cousin of the King's youngest wife, fled with the sole surviving heir to the throne—five-year-old Christmas Savungi."

Jack's fist tensed; his eyes shot to Cass.

His commander continued in his trademark staccato voice. "Tsabatu has been found dead in her home, along with cameraman Samuel Sekibo. A CBN foreign correspondent, Cass Rousseau, was seen leaving the U.S. residential compound with Sekibo yesterday, during the evacuation. Is she the one with you?" he demanded. "Does she have the king?"

Jack's skin chilled under his perspiration, his gaze falling to the wide-eyed boy eating his MRE.

Christmas was the new king of Kigali?

He cursed to himself, his attention shifting to Cass who was watching him intently, her entire body wire-tense. Damn her—*she knew!*

"If you have the boy, Bannister, I need you to stand down stat, remain exactly where you are until I receive orders directly from Joint Chiefs of Staff in Washington, because Zuma has issued a statement saying that if the U.S. is harboring the king, he will consider it an act of war on the part of the United States and all its European allies. He will start by killing the American staff at a diamond mine he has already taken hostage in the south. A staff of seventy. General Zuma will also give orders that any foreign national should be slain on sight."

Jeezus, this was about to blow. There could be hundreds of foreign nationals still stationed in Kigali. Jack glowered at Cass. She knew exactly who Christmas was and she never told him. She had not trusted him enough.

"I repeat, Warrant Officer Bannister, *do* you have the boy?"

Chapter 10

December 24, 0702 Zulu

Conflict churned inside Jack. He was sweltering under the heat as the day's temperatures rose and seconds ticked. The Ivory Coast border was still a nightmarish trek ahead, up over the ridge through increasingly steep and treacherous terrain. It would take at least another day. He gripped his radio, every muscle in his body strung wire-tight as he fumed at Cass. Two hot spots began to ride high on her cheeks. And bitterness pooled in his gut—he had no doubt at all that she'd known all along.

She'd tricked him into this corner.

And now he had one of the biggest decisions of his life to make.

She mouthed "no," shaking her head, eyes wide. She'd deduced what Jack was being asked. "Please, Jack," she whispered.

Jack tried to swallow the ball of rage growing hard

and painful in his throat. She'd lied. A lie of incredible magnitude.

She'd dared to ask for his help, but had not trusted him enough to tell him the whole story. And it had landed him bang in the middle of an international diplomatic powder keg. She'd forced him to make sacrifices, and she hadn't come clean herself. Jack felt duped. Used. The anger swelled up from his stomach, all the more fierce because he'd kissed her. He'd fallen deep, fast and hard, again—dared to hope for a future, and she had just blown it all out the water.

Then Jack's gaze fell to Christmas, clutching tight at Cass's pants. He felt a squeeze in his heart and a raw protective power surged into him. Zuma or his men—if they ever got their hands on the boy—would slaughter that child on the spot.

Could he allow this five-year-old child to become a pawn in Zuma's game with the White House?

Now that he'd come this far, could he remain here and wait to see if he was forced to hand the boy over?

And in spite of it all, in spite of his anger, his sense of betrayal, Jack was drawn further over the line of no return, moving insidiously from soldier—a role that had always defined him—to renegade.

He sucked in a deep breath. "No," he said firmly to his commander. "I have Cass Rousseau, but there is no boy."

He keyed off, lurched toward her, fury powering his body. He jabbed his finger at her face. "You," he yelled, "have pushed me into this—you forced my hand and you didn't even have the decency to give me the truth!"

She swallowed. "Jack—"

"I trusted you, Cass. By God, one thing I always did was trust you with the truth, goddammit! You were always *about* the truth...seeking it in your stories. Or so you led me to believe. And you lied to me—*used* me. And now? Look what you've done—you've hammered the nails in my coffin! I'll be court-martialed when this gets out. I'm going to prison. Do you really understand what this means, what you have asked from me here? Do you not understand what I am doing for you…for *Jacob?*"

Both froze.

There, it had been said. It was out in the open.

And the vocalization was so powerful it rocked them both, taking on a sentient power of its own, swirling around them. Blood drained from his face. She swayed slightly. Then, galvanized, she hit back, everything she'd ever buried coming out in an adrenalinized rush.

"Damn you, Jack. Who are *you* to talk about sacrifice? You don't make sacrifices for your family. You're all about your troops, duty to the flag and country over your marriage."

"That is not true—and it's not fair!"

"You were the one who missed Jacob's birth! And his first birthday. You were the one would couldn't be there on our wedding anniversary, or for Christmas four years ago, because of a tour you didn't have to accept."

"I had to accept that mission—"

"No, you did not. It was for a career move. If you'd been there, maybe…maybe I wouldn't have taken that Alaska assignment, and I wouldn't have had to take Jacob with me—"

"Don't go there, Cass," he warned, eyes narrowing.

"Oh, why not? You're the one who said I was running from facing it. Let me face you now! Maybe Jacob would still be alive, Jack, if you had been home."

He spun away from her.

Cass's eyes filled with hot tears. "Look at me, Jack!"

He did. White-faced, furious, his fists balling at his sides. "How dare you say that? How can you honestly believe it?"

"Because when we had to move to North Carolina I was forced to turn down *my* promotion, and find yet another job, with yet another station, and almost immediately you went off on another tour. It was that new station that assigned me the Alaska piece, and I didn't want to leave Jacob with some stranger over Christmas, so I had to take him with to cover the assignment—"

"The storm wasn't my fault, Cass."

"We wouldn't have been on that plane."

Silence simmered. Water trickled close by. Shrieks and cries called through the jungle.

"This is not fair, Cass," he whispered.

"You know it's true, Jack."

"You can't do this. You can't look back with what-ifs. What happened, happened, okay? We needed to deal with that, move forward. *Together.*"

"How could I move forward! You blamed me for taking him with me!"

"It was a knee-jerk reaction, Cass, and I am so sorry—I was in shock. I'd just returned home from Afghanistan to learn you were in the hospital, almost died, the sole survivor of a plane crash...my son gone...I..."

He sat, slumping onto a log, and he scrubbed his face in his hands. "I'm so sorry, Cass. I...didn't know how to deal." Jack sat, silent, gathering himself. "I didn't know how to handle my own guilt. My own sorrow for not having been there for you both. For making so many mistakes. So I hit out instead. If you'd only hung on long enough to let me work through it... long enough to allow me to say I was sorry."

He got up, took her hands in his, eyes locked with hers. "But you ran away. You chucked those five years of our marriage, your ring, you boxed up all the photos, all our precious memories, and you shipped them into storage, all after one major fight, and you took off for the first international hot spot you could find. And you haven't stopped running since. Look at you, Cass, you're thin. You're tired. You're drained."

"So I look like crap."

"And I love you more than ever."

Her eyes flickered.

"It wasn't just that one fight, Jack," she said, very quietly. "It was the last straw."

"It wasn't a straw—it was the *death of our son*. It was almost losing you. I came home to all that news. It was a shock. You didn't give me a chance to—"

"You were the one who hit back at me saying I wasn't cut

out to be a military wife," she said, voice thick with emotion. "And you were right, Jack. I'm not. I couldn't—*can't*—compete with your loyalty to your country."

"Yet now you're forcing me to give it all up anyway—to face a court-martial, prison, dishonorable discharge."

She scrubbed her hands over her face.

He turned away, inhaling deeply.

Then he felt a small tug at his camo pants, and glanced down—Christmas, his eyes huge and frightened by their yelling. And for another insane, upside-down second, he saw Jacob again. It was as if their son was reaching out from some spiritual realm, touching them both. Jack shook off the odd chill, glanced at Cass. And by the look in her eyes, he knew she'd felt it too.

"Mr. Jack, can we go now?"

Jack blew out a chest full of air, feeling like a cad. This child had been through so much, how could he have allowed himself, even for one second, to forget why he'd come down this jungle path. He touched the boy's head, said in Kigali. "You are right, my little man. We need to move."

Chapter 11

December 24, 1745 Zulu

In heavy silence, they trekked for miles, the terrain growing steeper, more slippery, vines tangling over rocks drenched in moss.

Jack stopped, gave them each a mug of water sterilized with tabs from his kit. It was almost night. "We'll try to keep moving in the dark," he said, packing their mugs away. "For as long as we can."

Darkness fell as they were crossing a river, the moon beginning to glint on the water's surface. Cass heard the terrifying sound of a crocodile splashing, and in her nervousness she slipped. Quickly the current sucked her downriver. The sound of a waterfall thundered below.

"Don't move!" Jack yelled at Christmas as he dropped the pack and weapons and plunged into the water after Cass.

She caught a branch and he managed to pull her out, dripping, shaking. He helped her back along the bank to where Christmas waited, and they slumped to the ground. Jack held her, just held, until he felt the tension in her body releasing. Pushing the wet hair back from her face, he looked down into her eyes. They caught the moonlight from a gap in the canopy above. "You could have trusted me, Cass," he said, his need suddenly so raw he couldn't take it anymore. "You could have told me the truth. We could have embarked on this journey as a team."

"If I had told you, Jack, what would you have done? Would have informed the DCM, your commander?"

He dragged his hand over his own wet hair. "I don't know, Cass. I honestly don't know anything anymore. The kid's a political time bomb, yet there's no way I could hand him over. To either side, not without being able to guarantee his well-being." He sucked in a deep breath of air. "I don't even know who I am, anymore. I…" He snorted a laugh. "I lost myself when I lost you. I guess I've been looking ever since."

Cass's eyes burned. Selfishness was something she'd always accused him of. Now she could see what she'd done to Jack, through her own self-absorption.

And his gut honesty was raw, new to her. Her powerful special ops soldier was suddenly rendered vulnerable in some way. He *needed* her.

Not just physically, but in some much deeper, more human way.

It's why he carried the photo. It's why he still wore his ring. It's why he was doing this.

"Jack," she said quietly. "I didn't tell you because I didn't want to force you to choose between helping me and your duty. We've been down that road…it didn't work."

Jack sat silent for a while beside her, watching Christmas squeeze the rest of the meal ration out the packet. This flight to freedom might have precipitated an identity crisis in him, but he was beginning, very clearly, in this dark and murky jungle, to see exactly who he wanted to be.

And just how far he was truly prepared to go to make it happen.

"You know, I think I made that choice some time ago, Cass," he said quietly.

Before I even came to Kigali.

"I vowed to myself that if I ever got a second chance with you, I'd do it differently. I'd be older, wiser and I'd know better. I chose you, Cass. Now we're in this together. To the hilt. And I hope to hell you're going to choose me, stick by me, and go all the way. Across that border. But I need your trust, Cass. One hundred percent. I need you to make your own sacrifice."

Emotion pulled her beautiful features, pale in the silver moonlight, her eyes dark, tired pools. And he wanted her. All of her, naked in his arms.

"You have to promise you will continue to lie about Christmas for as long as it takes to keep him safe, even when we get over that border. Promise me there will be no big insider feature story, no television interviews. No mention of the little king surviving at all. No matter how big this story of Kigali grows, you have to give it up."

He was asking her to stop being a journalist, just like he'd been forced to go renegade.

"I did that already, Jack, when I stopped observing the news and started making a difference." Tears spilled, suddenly unstoppable. Jack gathered her into his arms, held, comforted, and Cass sobbed every last sob she had not let out since her son's death.

He stroked her hair. Loving her. She was finally letting it go. And he was helping her. They were doing this together. Making the compromises they should have made a long time ago, for their family. For their child.

She looked up, finally spent. "I love you, Jack," she whispered.

His own eyes filled with emotion and his heart jackhammered. "Christmas will be safe because of Jacob, Cass," he whispered against her cheek, her ear, tasting her tears, his whole world cracking open, making him vulnerable to loss once again.

But he had to go there if he wanted her back.

"He'll live because our Jacob died. Because we came together."

She nodded, wiping her nose, smiling wanly through her tears. "We'll do it, we'll make it."

"Okay, we'll set up camp here, sleep for a few hours, and by tomorrow morning we should be through."

But that belief was instantly shattered as Jack spied a faint flicker of light in the forest valley miles below. He grabbed his night-vision scope and swore. He could make out twenty men entering dense jungle, all wearing either a red beret, headband or armband. They carried industrial-strength spotlights, machetes, machine guns.

"They're on our track," he whispered, pulse kicking. "Somehow they must know we have the king!"

"What now?"

Jack fired a glance at Christmas. "Now we run."

"In the dark? On this steep terrain?"

Jack looked up, and through the small gap in the canopy, a single bright star had moved into his line of vision. He realized suddenly, it was Christmas Eve.

"Yes, through this terrain," he whispered. "We follow that star, and we believe."

Chapter 12

December 24, 2100 Zulu

Jack worked his way up a frake tree almost two hundred feet tall. Using his night-vision scope, he scanned the jungle valley below, but saw nothing more. Wherever those men had gone, a dark canopy now hid them.

But he tensed suddenly, panning back as he caught a faint glimmer through the foliage. His chest tightened—they were gaining fast with their huge spotlights, moving with a dogged and lethal sense of purpose. They probably had an expert jungle tracker with them as well, someone who knew this terrain like he never could.

He checked his watch, GPS. The border was still some miles out and moving farther in this darkness would be really dangerous. However, if they hid and waited for dawn, Jack had little doubt they'd be tracked down like sitting ducks within the next few hours.

His only hope in saving the boy was to keep going, as fast as they possibly could. There was one other option, but it was not something Jack wanted to contemplate, not with a small child to bear witness.

He shimmied down the tree, landing with a soft thump. Cass immediately touched his arm in the darkness. "Is everything okay?" Jack cupped her neck, firm, reassuring. "Everything's fine," he lied. "We're doing great. As long as we keep moving."

"Christmas is shivering, Jack. He's stressed. I—"

Jack lowered himself to the child's eye level, took both his little shoulders in his hands, and he spoke in Kigali. "It's Christmas Eve, do you know that?"

He shook his head.

"When we get a bit higher, up on that ridge over there, the forest canopy will be thin, and if you look up you will see one very bright star in the east. It's the same star that, many, many years ago, guided three wise kings to a small manger and a little baby born on Christmas Day." Jack made it up as he went—he had no idea which star it really had been, hadn't ever really thought about it. But he felt the tension in the child's body ease as he spoke, so he kept talking, conscious of the precious seconds slipping by.

"Tell me," he said quietly to the boy, "how did you get your name, Christmas?"

The child was silent for several beats, and more seconds ticked by. Jack could almost sense the intent of the soldiers coming towards them.

"My mother," he finally whispered in Kigali. "She likes Christmas Day."

Emotion ripped through Jack—the child still spoke of his mother in the present tense. He did not yet know that he'd lost his entire family.

Jack had to pause to gather himself, to not project any negativity in his voice. "And why does she like it?"

"My mother says there is goodness at this time. People must remember to be kind to each other. And…it is my birthday."

Jack flattened his mouth, thinking about the crowded shopping malls and hysteria back home, the fake fat Santas, the piles of presents and all the commercials for toys and food and clothes, but here, in this dark jungle, stripped to the basics, the true meaning of the season was being spoken in the innocent words of a child, on Christmas Eve.

It was about humanity. Love.

And more than ever, for completely different reasons than when he started on this desperate flight into the jungle encrusted hills, Jack wanted to make things right for this child. Not just save him—but show him that humanity *could* be kind, to find a way to give the child the faith he would need in the days to come. To show him that a soldier could be good.

Even if he didn't follow orders.

"What did he say?" Cass whispered, squatting down beside Jack and the boy.

"He..." Emotion hitched his voice. "He said tomorrow is his birthday." Jack paused, gathering himself. "We're going to get him across that border, Cass, goddammit," he said, eyes burning. "He's going to turn six tomorrow, and we're going to make damn sure of it."

"I'm glad we're here, Jack," Cass whispered against his ear, her lips brushing his cheek with a soft kiss. "Because even if we don't make it, it gave me a chance to see who you really are. It reminded me why I really have always loved you."

For the first time Jack was glad the night was black as a pitch—no one could see the soldier's tear that leaked from the corner of his eye.

He put his arm around Cass, took Christmas's hand. And he led them into the dark, steep jungle. Together.

December 24, 2145 Zulu

Jack swung his machete, skin glazed with sweat as they burst through tangled vines and dense understory onto the ridge. Cass caught her breath. Savannah grasses blew gently in hot wind between tall trees, the scene silvered by clusters of stars that formed a bright band of light spanning the heavens. Never had she seen anything so beautiful.

Cass halted for a second, falling back, stunned by the magnitude of the celestial wonder, the surreal sense that they were part of something bigger, a planet, a world. A universe. Then she caught sight of one bright, shining star to the east.

The star Jack had told Christmas to look out for.

Star of wonder, star of light...emotion balled in her throat. It was like she'd been given a vision, a new way to see. And she felt the presence of her son. With the feeling came a deep sense of peace, as if she could finally let Jacob—and the physical pain she felt over losing him—go. She was finally allowing herself to remember Jacob, the good times, without the accompanying crushing guilt, the fear that she was betraying him somehow if she wasn't hurting at the same time.

Tears of release streamed down her face. Exhaustion, she told herself. She was fatigued, being ridiculously emotional, but in lagging behind Jack and Christmas, things had fallen strangely still. And in the unnatural silence, she heard a noise, carrying up through the forest behind her. Cass tensed, listening. It was a voice—she heard it again. And the sound of rocks clattering down the gorge they'd just climbed

She stumbled ahead. "Jack!" she hissed, grabbing his arm. "They're right behind us!"

He swore, checking his GPS, a green glow in the dark. "We're still a quarter-mile out—we're not going to make it, Cass."

"What do we do?"

The one thing he didn't want to do.

Chapter 13

December 24, 2150 Zulu

It was almost midnight and a strange silence hung in the humidity. Even the wind and crickets had fallen quiet.

Jack had hidden Christmas inside the rotten trunk of a monstrous kapok tree. He'd covered the entrance with thick vines and told Christmas not to move, not to come out, not even to try and peep through the vine curtain, because light might glance off his eyes, and someone might see him.

He touched his head of dark tight curls. "I will come and get you when it is safe," he whispered. "We will cross the border and then tomorrow, when the sun comes up, it will be your birthday."

He nodded. "Thank you, Mr. Jack. I will be happy for that. And to see my mother."

The words tore through Jack's chest like something physical, and the voice sounded so like Jacob's for a moment. Crap, he must be tired. This whole business of timing—his wedding anniversary, the season of Jacob's death. This child called

Christmas who'd come into his life like a haunting little guardian angel to lead him and Cass down a twisting path into their past, and into the jungle…it was all playing tricks with his mind, he thought as he made his way to the clearing where Cass was hiding in the grass with his assault rifle and one of his knives.

Jack swung himself up into a tree, vines dangling down around him. With him he had his knife, machete and side-arm.

Sweat beaded along his brow as he waited, ready like a jungle cat, ears attuned to the deathly silence.

Cass, on the other hand, heard only the boom of blood pounding in her ears. Her entire body was wet with perspiration, her hands shaking. She was no stranger to shooting—she'd done survival courses, put in her time at ranges. She'd wanted to be prepared for anything a war or disaster zone might throw at her.

But an assault weapon was unfamiliar.

And she'd never killed a man.

Never even aimed at one.

Aim to kill, Cass, center of body mass, do not think, or you will be dead. Remember, it's them or us.

Jack's warning curled through her mind as she felt something crawl over the back of her leg. She fought the urge to move, prayed it wasn't a snake, scorpion or something equally deadly. The scent of grass was pungent where her body had crushed it and she could smell fear on herself, in her perspiration, taste it in her mouth. Sweat dribbled into her eyes.

She heard a rustle, and clacking of fat leaves, saw a flash of a light, then another as the men began to emerge. The cadre was moving swiftly and silently.

The tracker moved up front, ebony skin gleaming under the light of stars and slice of moon. He bent down, examined the grass, motioning for a second man to aim the big flashlight at the ground. He studied the ground, looking for tracks. His body stiffened. He looked up, held out three fingers.

Cass's pulse quickened. He knew they were here!

Did he suspect they were lying in wait to ambush them?

Through the long blades of grass she saw the tracker point to the left, showing two fingers one way, then one the other—in the direction of Christmas's hiding tree.

Cass swore to herself as men started running in a crouch, weapons leading, going the way Jack had taken Christmas. Now or never. Heart jackhammering, she squinted her eye, focusing on the center of mass of the dark shadows. Releasing her breath slowly, she squeezed the trigger.

Keeping her finger down she fired, moving across one shadow to the others.

The men shuddered, another yelled, immediately returning fire to her spot in the dark grass.

Cass gasped as bullets *thwocked* into the ground around her, one buzzing like a hornet past her ear. Then another man spun to face her, opened fire, but as he did, Jack dropped from above, taking him down with a thud as he slit his neck. It distracted the men enough for Cass, as she had been instructed, to rise up and fire again. This time she took another two men down before dropping back and rolling sideways into a gully as more slugs thudded and kicked up wet dirt around her.

She heard yelling, grunts. Thumping.

Then silence. Dead ominous silence.

"*Jack?*" she whispered.

No response.

Shaking like a leaf, covered in sweat and mud and grass and bits of leaf debris, Cass shakily got to her knees.

Nothing moved.

She could smell blood, the scent of fired weapons.

She tried to move, stumbling as her legs gave out under her. She crawled, got up again, walked like a pile of jelly to the motionless bodies.

She could make out Jack's arm under one of the big men.

And in that moment…under the vast, starlit African sky, Cass knew she'd move mountains to save Jack, and to have a second chance, a future with him. *Please dear God, just let him be alive.*

She could not lose him now, not after having endured this strange flight through the Kigali jungle. She walked in a crouch, coming closer to the pile of men, knife at the ready in front of her, muscles shaking. She felt the neck of the first man—no pulse.

"Jack!" she hissed, eyes burning as she tried to heft the dead weight off him.

Underneath Jack lay still. Blood gleamed, black and shining, across his face and along a slash in his arm.

She dropped to her knees, lifting his head into her lap, pressing her palm firmly against the gaping wound on his arm, trying to stop the bleeding. "Oh, God, Jack."

He moaned.

Her heart kicked, slammed. Hope—all the hope she'd ever lost suddenly burned furnace-bright, searing back through her body and soul, energy crackling into her. "Jack, can you hear me?" She wiped blood from his face, his eyes, trying to keep a firm grip on his wound, blood coming out from between her fingers.

He groaned again, and smiled. "You look like an angel."

Relief punched through her. "Yeah. Right—I'm sure. One bloody angel. You get a knock on the head or what?"

He put his left hand to his temple. "Must've been concussed, out for a moment."

"Put pressure here." She moved his hand onto his arm, then took her knife, cutting through his sleeve to make ribbons of fabric. Fevered urgency drove her movements as she bound them tight in a bandage on his arm.

"Christmas?"

"They didn't get anywhere near him. Hurry up, hold this. I'll go find him."

"No," he crawled to his feet wobbled. "Wait. Help me. I'll show you where he is—you won't find him on your own."

Arm over her shoulder, his weight heavy, Cass and Jack stumbled together through thick grass. The sudden aftereffects of adrenaline shuddered through her. She had to stop a moment and throw up, arms braced against a tree.

"You okay, Cass?"

She nodded. Wiping her sleeve over her mouth. "I've never killed anyone." Tears began to stream down her cheeks as violent shaking took hold.

"You saved my life, Cass. You did good." He lifted her chin. "Look at me."

She did.

"We saved Christmas. Look, up there."

The star.

"It's almost midnight," he whispered. "We go in the direction of that star and we can get him over that border before his sixth birthday. It's only a quarter-mile. We can do this."

They gathered themselves, found the kapok giant, bent down, opened the vine curtain. Two shining eyes looked out of the darkness. Jack opened his arms and Christmas lurched into them.

Cass saw tears on her soldier's face.

They carried the small boy through the savannah grasses growing high in a strip cleared for border patrol, a no-man's-land between Ivory Coast and Kigali.

Spotlights suddenly swung onto them, and an order was barked for them to stand still. Soldiers approached with weapons pointed at them.

Cass and Jack put their hands in the air and Jack called out in the native language. "We come in peace!" he yelled. "We need help for a small boy!"

More spots flared to them. A jeep engine started, and there was yelling as more troops emerged and men encircled them.

"Must've heard your shooting," he whispered to Cass. "They were waiting for us."

"United States Army?" A huge man in a maroon beret demanded, scanning Jack's military gear.

"I got separated from my team while evacuating the embassy of the United States," he said, knowing the Ivory Coast government was sympathetic and had organized a staging area near the ocean.

"Who is the child?"

"The child is an orphan from a small village. He needs medical attention. We need to get him to the U.S. staging camp."

"And the woman?"

He turned, looked at Cass. "This woman," Jack said, "is my wife."

Chapter 14

December 25, 0555 Zulu

After the Cote d'Ivoire army medic had taken a look at Christmas, treated his dehydration and tended to Jack's wounds and Cass's cuts, they'd put Christmas to bed in a cot in one of the military tents at the border camp. With the help of a sedative, he'd gone down like a little log.

They'd all be flown to the U.S. staging base later in the morning.

Meanwhile, Cass and Jack sat next to a fire in the camp, sipping brandy one of the soldiers had poured for them. In silence they watched the African dawn arriving along the horizon in a violent streak of orange. The sounds of the jungle rose in a raucous crescendo as the daylight crept over the land. Far below on the plain, three giraffes ran along a curving, coffee-brown river.

Jack reached for Cass's hand. "Remember how different it looked for us Christmas Day nine years ago?"

She felt his warmth, the ring. Nine years ago, Christmas

Day, they'd been on their honeymoon in the Colorado Rockies, snowbound in a small lodge, a fire crackling in the room.

Lights had twinkled on a real fir.

They'd made love in front of the fire.

The scent, she remembered it well—real log fire, pine needles. Jack. The fresh cotton sheets. The croissants, coffee.

She remembered how Jack had stroked the small swell of her pregnant tummy.

Cass closed her eyes, allowing it all to wash over her. Her eyes filled with moisture and her heart hurt, but it was a beautiful hurt. Jack had shown her that she needn't have been so afraid of this kind of hurt.

She tightened her fingers around Jack's. "Yes," she whispered, "I remember. Every little detail."

He squeezed her hand back. Thinking how warm and naked she'd been in his arms. And how ironic that even with all those trappings of Christmas back home, he'd never quite understood the true meaning of it all, and of life, until now, here under this African dawn, on this particular Christmas Day.

How incredible that something so beautiful, something so pure, so right, could grow out of the darkness they'd fled.

"I've missed you, Cass. God, I've missed you."

Jack saw the tears glistening on her cheeks, and his chest ached with love, poignant happiness. Somehow they'd both redeemed themselves. Somehow this trip through the jungle had helped them both accept their losses and their mistakes. And it had brought them back together. In a stronger bond than ever, a more adult one.

"Do you think we could try again, Cass, one day, one small step at a time?"

She was silent for a long moment, watching a flock of pelicans fly over the trees. "Why are you really here, Jack," she answered with a question of her own. "In Africa?"

He knew what she was asking. She was thinking it had to be more than mere coincidence that he'd been posted to Kigali. He turned away, sat silent for a long time, watching the sky change. "Because I knew you were here," he said quietly. "And I could never quite let you go. I put in for this tour." He paused. "Hell knows, Cass, maybe I just wanted to be near. Maybe...I thought I could save you. From yourself. For myself. Mostly I wanted a second chance."

Emotion thickened Cass's throat as she felt that warm gold wedding band of promise, a reminder of her hope, on his finger, and she thought about that crumpled photo in his breast pocket. He'd never given up when she had.

That was Jack, stubborn to a fault. And she loved him for it, faults and all.

"I'd like that," she whispered. "More than anything." She hesitated. "And Jack...I'm sorry. For everythi—" He placed two fingers on her lips.

"Shh," he said. "We take with us only the good memories from now, and we move forward."

She nodded, tears rolling down her cheeks.

He tilted her chin up, the gold sunlight catching her skin, painting her hair flax, and they kissed as Christmas Day dawned bright in the African jungle, amidst a rising cacophony of sounds as raw and magical and more beautiful right now than any Christmas carol Jack had ever heard.

He stood, taking her hand, lifting her to her feet, and he led her back to the tent, where they made love.

Somehow in saving Christmas, the little boy had in turn brought hope, a second chance, and he'd saved them.

* * * * *

COMING NEXT MONTH

Available October 26, 2010

ROMANTIC SUSPENSE

REQUEST YOUR FREE BOOKS!

2 FREE NOVELS
PLUS
2 FREE GIFTS!

▼ *Silhouette*®

ROMANTIC
SUSPENSE

Sparked by Danger, Fueled by Passion.

YES! Please send me 2 FREE Silhouette® Romantic Suspense novels and my 2 FREE gifts (gifts are worth about $10). After receiving them, if I don't wish to receive any more books, I can return the shipping statement marked "cancel." If I don't cancel, I will receive 4 brand-new novels every month and be billed just $4.24 per book in the U.S. or $4.99 per book in Canada. That's a saving of 15% off the cover price! It's quite a bargain! Shipping and handling is just 50¢ per book.* I understand that accepting the 2 free books and gifts places me under no obligation to buy anything. I can always return a shipment and cancel at any time. Even if I never buy another book from Silhouette, the two free books and gifts are mine to keep forever.

240/340 SDN E5Q4

Name	(PLEASE PRINT)	
Address		Apt. #
City	State/Prov.	Zip/Postal Code

Signature (if under 18, a parent or guardian must sign)

Mail to the **Silhouette Reader Service:**
IN U.S.A.: P.O. Box 1867, Buffalo, NY 14240-1867
IN CANADA: P.O. Box 609, Fort Erie, Ontario L2A 5X3

Not valid for current subscribers to Silhouette Romantic Suspense books.

Want to try two free books from another line?
Call 1-800-873-8635 or visit www.morefreebooks.com.

* Terms and prices subject to change without notice. Prices do not include applicable taxes. N.Y. residents add applicable sales tax. Canadian residents will be charged applicable provincial taxes and GST. Offer not valid in Quebec. This offer is limited to one order per household. All orders subject to approval. Credit or debit balances in a customer's account(s) may be offset by any other outstanding balance owed by or to the customer. Please allow 4 to 6 weeks for delivery. Offer available while quantities last.

Your Privacy: Silhouette is committed to protecting your privacy. Our Privacy Policy is available online at www.eHarlequin.com or upon request from the Reader Service. From time to time we make our lists of customers available to reputable third parties who may have a product or service of interest to you. If you would prefer we not share your name and address, please check here. ☐

Help us get it right—We strive for accurate, respectful and relevant communications. To clarify or modify your communication preferences, visit us at www.ReaderService.com/consumerchoice.

SRS10R

HARLEQUIN®

A Romance

FOR EVERY MOOD™

Spotlight on

Inspirational

Wholesome romances
that touch the heart and soul.

See the next page
to enjoy a sneak peek from
the Love Inspired® Suspense
inspirational series.

*See below for a sneak peek from
our inspirational line, Love Inspired® Suspense*

*Enjoy this heart-stopping excerpt from
RUNNING BLIND
by top author Shirlee McCoy,
available November 2010!*

**The mission trip to Mexico was supposed to be an
adventure. But the thrill turns sour when Jenna Dougherty
and her roommate Magdalena are kidnapped.**

"It's okay. I'm here to help." The voice was as deep as the
darkness, but Jenna Dougherty didn't believe the lie. She
could do nothing but lie still as hands slid down her arms,
felt the rope around her wrists.

"I'm going to use a knife to cut you free, Jenna. Hold
still."

The cold blade of a knife pressed close to her head before
her gag fell away.

"I—" she started, but her mouth was dry, and she could
do nothing but suck in air.

"Shhh. Whatever needs to be said can be said when
we're out of here." Nick spoke quietly, his hand gentle on
her cheek. There and gone as he sliced through the ropes on
her wrists and ankles.

He pulled her upright. "Come on. We may be on
borrowed time."

"I can't leave my friend," Jenna rasped out.

"There's no one here. Just us."

"She has to be here." Jenna took a step away.

"There's no one here. Let's go before that changes."

"It's dark. Maybe if we find a light…"

"What did you say?"

"We need to turn on the light. I can't leave until I know that—"

"What can you see, Jenna?"

"Nothing."

"No shadows? No light?"

"No."

"It's broad daylight. There's light spilling in from the window I climbed in through. You can't see it?"

She went cold at his words.

"I can't see anything."

"You've got a nasty bruise on your forehead. Maybe that has something to do with it." His fingers traced the tender flesh on her forehead.

"It doesn't matter *how* it happened. I'm blind!"

Can Nick help Jenna find her friend or will chasing this trail have Jenna running blindly again into danger?

Find out in RUNNING BLIND, available in November 2010 only from Love Inspired Suspense.